JAN 2011

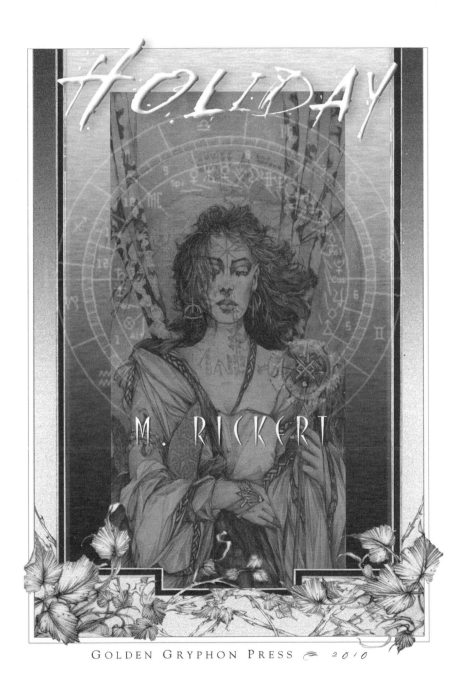

HOLIDAY

M. RICKERT

GOLDEN GRYPHON PRESS ❧ 2010

Introduction, copyright © 2010 by M. Rickert.
"Holiday," first published in *Subterranean Magazine* #7, 2007.
"Memoir of a Deer Woman," first published in *Fantasy and Science Fiction*, March 2007.
"Journey into the Kingdom," first published in *Fantasy and Science Fiction*, May 2006.
"The Machine," first published in *Fantasy and Science Fiction*, January 2003.
"Evidence of Love in a Case of Abandonment: One Daughter's Personal Account," first published in *Fantasy and Science Fiction*, Oct/Nov 2008.
"Don't Ask," first published in *Fantasy and Science Fiction*, December 2007.
"Traitor," first published in *Fantasy and Science Fiction*, May 2008.
"Was She Wicked? Was She Good?", copyright © 2010 by M. Rickert.
"You Have Never Been Here," first published in *Feeling Very Strange: The Slipstream Anthology*, ed. James Patrick Kelly & John Kessel, Tachyon Publications, 2006.
"War is Beautiful," first published in *Flytrap* #9, June 2008.
"The Christmas Witch," first published in *Fantasy and Science Fiction*, December 2006.

Copyright © 2010 by M. Rickert

LIBRARY OF CONGRESS CATALOGING–IN–PUBLICATION DATA

Rickert, M. (Mary), 1959–
   Holiday / M. Rickert. — 1st ed.
     p.   cm.
   ISBN-13: 978-1-930846-65-4 (alk. paper)
   ISBN-10: 1-930846-65-7 (alk. paper)
    I. Title.
PS3618.I375   H65   2010
813'.6—dc22
                     2010026768

Printed in the United States of America.
First Edition.

Contents

Dedicated to my Mom, Kathleen Rickert, for listening to my stories before anyone else would.

"Sometimes our inner light goes out, but it is blown again into flame by an encounter with another human being. Each of us owes the deepest thanks to those who have rekindled this inner light."
—Albert Schweitzer

With Gratitude To:

Marie Angkum
Chris Barzak
Bill Bauerband
Rick Bowes
Tom Canty
Karen Crandall
Douglas Glover
Marcia Gorra-Patek
Dr. Jacki Irland
Dr. Gary Lewis
Stephen King
Mary Leonard
The Lyons Family
Howard Morhaim
Liz Musser
My Family
Joyce Carol Oates
Peter Straub
Terry Schuster
Thomas and Patty Tunney
Gary Turner
Gordon Van Gelder
Gary Wolfe

♦ ♦ ♦

Introduction

I TURNED FIFTY THIS YEAR AND REALIZED THAT I no longer need to look to the future, the way I did when I was younger, for resource or inspiration. Much of my youth was invested in becoming a writer, which seemed a mysterious and uncertain process; only recently, looking at the friends I have grown with (and googling some who passed my way) have I discovered that the formula for becoming is not as complicated as I once thought it was. Almost everyone, I realized, became what they worked at becoming. Is it really that easy? Well, yes, and no. The challenge of youth is that terrible space of the unknown, and I spent many uncomfortable years believing in the fantasy of my future, while working as a maid, a bookstore clerk, a coffee shop barista; believing that one day I would be a writer, when all around me there was no evidence of that beyond my belief, and the fact that I wrote.

I left home at eighteen, announcing my plans to write the great American novel, and traveled across the country to California, where I joined my older sister. It never occurred to me that she wouldn't be absolutely thrilled with my arrival. Not that I necessarily thought she would be thrilled either. We were family, of course we would offer each other shelter. I took my first plane ride, ruminating at the course of clouds, and the beginning of the exciting adventure of my life, and so arrived, with no idea how to cross a city street, how to prepare anything beyond scrambled eggs, and really no idea at all of how to become a writer other than to write. Before I left the home I had grown up in, I wrote a tender obituary for myself, and placed it where it was meant to be found in a timely manner should I die in a plane crash, as I was fairly certain would happen.

The fifty-year-old woman knows what the eighteen-year-old girl did not. Such a leaving is a kind of death, and that long plane ride marked my exit from the life of girl.

That year, my sister went back to Wisconsin for Christmas and I spent my first major holiday alone. Banking on my previous career as a baby sitter, I was, by then, working as a pre-school teacher. We got a small bonus for Christmas, something like fifteen or twenty-five dollars. On my way home from the bus stop I bought a Christmas tree. I didn't have a stand, or money for one, so the nice man hammered four pieces of wood into the trunk of the tree, warning me not to put lights on it, as it would dry out soon. To this I solemnly agreed. I carried my tree home and set it in the humble living room. I made ornaments out of flour, water, and salt. I lit candles on a nearby table. I remember being very lonely, and very sad. I can tie the unraveling of who I thought I was, to whom I became, and the terrible tangle of poor decisions in between, to that first Christmas spent alone.

My story is a very American story. I recognize the privilege of my sorrow, yet cannot escape the truth of it. I was sad and lonely, and if not rags poor, I was without funds, a living Christmas story. Not the one about the baby, but the one about the shop girl, the one about the mysterious angel at the door, the gift of love, the true meaning of Christmas. I still have a few of those bread dough ornaments, fashioned out of my belief in the power of a decorated tree. When I hang them now, I think of the girl I was with tenderness. Yes, her sorrows were, for the most part, privileges, and yes, it all turns out good in the end; she becomes a writer, she learns to appreciate Christmas in solitude, but she did not know this at the time, and yet she fashioned, to the best of her ability, a holiday of sorts.

Holidays, simply because there are less of them in any one person's life than the days that compose that life, because they tend to arrive with expectations, whether those expectations are met or not, whether there is even an attempt to meet them or not, offer the solace of memory, proof of existence even in the space of time that is otherwise lost. When I unpack my Christmas decorations, and once again hold one of those oddly painted, poorly formed ornaments, I travel back in time to the girl I was. That girl kept waiting for life to turn into a musical. Intellectually, she knew better, but she couldn't help herself, she had every intention of having a grand life, and in all the grand lives she had known, people broke out into song.

This did not happen, of course, and she adjusted to it. I remember her so well, this girl I was, because I can still hold the hope she made in the shape of a flour, salt, and water ornament, but why does this memory matter?

At fifty, I have likely, not necessarily, but quite likely, lived more of my life than I have left to live. Time is getting shorter now. For youth it seems, or at least for the youth I was, time is an arrow, but now it is something more like a Möbius strip. Holidays help to mark my days on that strip and because of them I am able to feel, not the diminishment of life, but its infinity.

Not everyone has happy holidays; the stories collected here are not, for the most part, what I would call happy. I am inclined not to call them sad either, though the reader is advised to take my assessment with the knowledge that it comes from someone who finds walking through graveyards quite inspiring. What these stories mean to do, limited as they are by the author's limitations, narrowed as they are by the author's acknowledgement of a narrow calendar of holidays, is to honor the experience of being human, an existence marked by countless forgotten hours, by hope for finding something that matters, by belief in celebrating time, though it is the body's nemesis. People sometimes find my stories strange, but what could be stranger than life? For me, I choose to celebrate the strange, the misshapen, the forgotten, even the inevitable death. For many people this is not what holidays are all about. For me, this is what everything is about.

M. Rickert
April 2010

Holiday

*S*HE SAYS HER NAME IS HOLIDAY, BUT I KNOW
she's lying. I remember her face. It was all over the news for
weeks, years even, but of course she doesn't know that. I briefly consider telling her, saying something like, "Hey, did you know you're
a star?" but that would necessitate bringing up the subject of her
death, and I'm not clear if she knows that she's a ghost, or that almost everyone thinks her parents killed her. That doesn't seem like
the kind of thing any kid should have to hear, so instead I say,
"Holiday? That's a pretty name."

Her body starts jerking in a strange way as she moves across my
bedroom floor, her arms held out, her hands moving to some secret
rhythm, and I think she's re-enacting her death, the way some ghosts
do, until I realize that she's tap dancing, her blonde curls bouncing,
that little-Miss smile plastered across her face, bright red like she
just finished eating a cherry Popsicle. I figured she came to tell me
who offed her, but instead she came to dance and tell me lies.

"Why don't you come here," I pat beside me on the bed. Just like
that she's gone. Like I'm a pervert or something. Poor dumb kid.

That's all there is until about a week later. This time I'm asleep on
the couch and she wakes me up, singing a country western song.

She's wearing a black cowboy hat with a big gold star on the front, a little black-and-red fringed skirt, a denim shirt with silver buttons, and red tasseled cowboy boots that come about halfway up her calves. She looks pretty cute. She's singing in the dulcet tone of someone twice her age, and right away I understand the confusion people felt about her, the strange aura of sexuality that comes off her and shouldn't. When she sees me watching, she waves, her little fingers slightly bent, but she doesn't miss a beat, even when she winks.

This is so freaking weird I don't know what to do so I wait until she's finished and then I applaud.

She curtsies, holding out the skirt with the tips of her tiny fingers; her perfect blonde curls undisturbed by her dance and song.

"So," I say, "Holiday, right?"

She nods, her red lips smirked.

"You hungry?" I pick up the half-full bag of Doritos on the coffee table in front of the couch and extend it toward her. She shakes her head. "Wanna watch a movie?" I ask. She just stands there, staring at me, squinting slightly, looking like she just might start crying, as though I have awoken her from some dream about Barbie dolls and Christmas and a perfect life, into this reality of being murdered and stuck, for all eternity, at age six, tap dancing forever. I look through my DVD collection, *Kill Bill* (1 and 2), *Seven Samurai*, *The Shining*, *Howard Stern's Private Parts* (severely underrated and under-appreciated, by the way), *City of Women*, *My Architect*, *Wild Weather Caught on Tape* (a gift from an old girlfriend) and *The Wet Women of California*, which, swear to God, I had forgotten all about. None of it exactly seems like the sort of thing to watch with a six-year-old murdered kid, so instead I turn on the TV and settle on the cooking channel, but I guess it wasn't the right choice because next thing I know, I'm sitting alone watching this chick with a giant smile, pouring liquid over hamburger meat. "Hey," I say to the air, "come back, we don't have to watch this." But of course no one answers and no one appears. I pick up one of the DVDs, and put it in, just to get rid of the headache I feel coming on. In two seconds, I'm watching naked, big-breasted women dive into the ocean, roll in the sand, and frolic with the waves and each other. I drink my warm beer and start to play with myself until I get the creepy feeling that maybe she's still in the room. I take my hand out of my pants, flick off the DVD, and turn over, my face pressed against the couch.

The next day I go to the library. There's a whole shelf devoted just to her. I page through the books and look at all the pictures.

Yep, it's her all right. I don't check out the books, just in case she comes back. I don't want her to see them and get scared or anything. I don't know why she's coming to see me, but I want her to come back. When I read about how her father found her, wrapped in a blanket, as though someone was worried she would be cold, but with that rope around her neck, and all the rest, I feel like something inside me wakes up, and it's not a completely disturbing feeling. I spend the whole day at the library and when I leave I'm tired, and hungry, but before I do anything else, I go to Wal-Mart and buy the boxed collection of Shirley Temple DVDs. They were her favorite. Next time she comes, I'm going to be prepared. Sarah Vehler, who was in my brother's class in high school, is the checkout girl. She's gained about five hundred pounds since then and I barely recognize her, but she recognizes me just fine. "I didn't know you have kids," she says. What am I supposed to do, tell her I've got a ghost? Instead, I just shrug. Maybe that was a mistake. I don't know. This was all new territory for me. I tried to do what was right.

When Terry, my agent, calls to see how the book is coming along, I tell him it's just fine. "But hey," I say, "I'm thinking of going in another direction, sort of."

"Shoot," Terry says.

I stumble around a bit and even though he's thousands of miles away, I know he's chewing his Nicotine gum faster and faster until finally he says, "Listen, just give it to me in a sentence, all right?"

"I wanna write about—" and I say her name.

"Who?"

For a long time she was everyone's little girl. The whole country followed her story and wanted vengeance for what was done to her, but now, hardly anyone even remembers her name.

"Oh, wait, the little Miss America kid, right? What's she got to do with anything? Did your parents know her parents or something?"

"Well, not exactly, but—"

"Don't blow this, okay? Memoir writing isn't what it used to be, all right? Just stick to the facts, make sure it's all documented."

"But I—"

"Stick to your own story. You got enough there to keep you busy, right?"

"But Terry," I say, "when I think about her, I mean, don't you think what happened to her was a real travesty?"

"Travesty? Right. Of course it was. But what happened to you was a real travesty too, wasn't it? Your whole family torn apart by false accusations, your father dying in prison for something he didn't do. That's the travesty you know. That's the one you can write about."

"I just think—"

"Okay, I know what's happening here. Something in your mind, in your sub-conscious is trying to distract you from writing this, am I right? Huh?"

"I guess," I say, glancing at my computer.

"Tell you what, why don't you just take a couple of days? Give yourself a break. Watch movies. Take walks in the park. Get laid. Take some time off, is what I'm saying, not weeks or anything but you know, take a few days, then you can come back to this all refreshed, okay?"

"Okay," I say.

"Who cares if you're a few days late, right?"

"Right."

"Just forget about the kid," he says. "She's not your story."

We say goodbye and I walk over to the computer and click on the file. I stare at the blank screen, certain that if I could just come up with the title, I could probably sail through the whole thing. But the title is ellusive. Instead I take Terry's advice and watch a movie, several in fact. Shirley Temple in black and white, highly, highly under-rated. I don't even know when she appears. But suddenly we are sitting on the couch, laughing. It feels so good to laugh like that I decide not to say anything. I don't want to scare her off. I don't know when she left. I fell asleep and when I woke up, she was gone.

The next day I sit staring at the screen on my computer for two hours, I know it sounds like an exaggeration, but I timed it. I try several titles. *My Father's Rules. I Am Not His Son. Rising Above the Prison He Resides In. Last Chance.* You get the picture, right? Crap. I click off the computer and take Terry's advice. I go to the park.

They are so young. So perfect, with their perfect skin and little teeth and they are dirty, and bratty, and crying, and laughing and completely absorbed by the sand in the sandbox, or the need to traverse the bars, dangling above the dangerous ground, holding tight, and it's obvious it hurts, but they are determined, stubborn, wild, beautiful. I could watch them for hours, but instead I just watch for a little while, I know too well what the grownups will think about someone like me, a young man, all alone, watching children play. I turn away, hunched against the sudden cold, walking slowly, soon no longer able to hear the laughter and the sound of their voices, shouting names, or shouting nonsense.

God, how I envy them.

When I get home my brother is standing on my porch, hunched into his jacket, his hands in his pockets. "Hey," he says.

"Hey," I say. "What's up?"

He shrugs, glances at my door, and then gives me that pretend smile of his.

"I don't have any," I say.

"What? Oh, that hurts bro," he says. "I'm sincerely hurt. I just thought, you know, I'd stop by."

I nod, but I do it with a smirk so that he knows I know the truth even if we are going to play this game. I take the key out of my pocket and let us into the house.

"Christ," he says.

"What?"

"Don't you ever clean up after yourself? Mom would shit if she saw this."

"Well, she's not going to see it, all right? We both know that. What do you want?"

He shrugs, but he's casing the joint. I'm a writer. I notice these things. "Man, I'm just so hurt, bro," he says. "What, you think I only come when—"

"Yeah," I say. "Yeah, I do."

We stand there, staring at each other, then he shrugs and walks into my living room, sits on the couch, I'm only half-paying attention, he picks up the remote control. "Wait," I say, but it's too late, Shirley Temple is dancing across the screen, all dimples and innocence.

I don't know what to do so I just stand there.

He's laughing so hard, he's bent over at the waist, and I start laughing too, and that's when he jumps up and grabs me by the collar and pushes me against the wall.

"I should fucking kill you," he says.

"It's not like that. I'm doing some research."

"Fucking pervert."

"I'm not the one," I say, only 'cause I'm desperate, only 'cause he's got this look in his eyes like he might really kill me.

He pushes me harder into the wall. He leans against me. "What did you say?"

"I'm not the one he liked most," I say and he lets go as if I'm on fire. For a moment we are just standing there, breathing heavy and staring at each other. I try to make it right. I reach over to touch his shoulder but he jerks away.

He wipes his hand through his hair, licks his lips, and then wipes them with the back of his hand, and his eyes stay cold.

"Come on," I try again.

He leans toward me, as if he would kill me if he could stand to touch me. He speaks, real slow, breathing onion into my face, "But you're the one who's grown up to be just like him."

"It's fucking research," I shout. He nods, like; sure, he doesn't believe me. He walks out of my house, my fucking addict brother, thinking he's got it all together and that I'm the one falling apart. I lock the door behind him, and when I turn, she's there, tap dancing across the kitchen in the outfit that caused all the controversy, the one with the feathers, and the black net stockings. "Oh, hi," I say, "did you catch any of that?"

She pirouettes in a furious twirl, a great flurry of tapping feet, and another twirl; I am sincerely amazed and clap until my hands feel raw. She smiles and smiles and then waves her arm, like a magician's assistant, and that's when I see the other little girl. She's taller, her skin is black, her hair in two ponytails high on her head, she's dressed just like a regular kid, a T-shirt, shorts, and flip-flops. "Hi," I say, "what's your name?"

She smiles, but it is a shy smile, her lips closed.

"Her name is Holiday too."

I nod, puzzling this out.

"And today is her birthday."

I turn to the girl who looks up at me with her beautiful black eyes.

"Your birthday?"

Both girls nod solemnly.

"Well, I don't, let me see what I can find. I wasn't expecting . . ." I rummage through the kitchen drawers and cabinets, making excuses all the while. "I wish I had known, I'm just so unprepared. A birthday? If I had known, I would have, I mean, balloons and cake . . ." The girls look up at me, bright-eyed, "but I'm sorry, I don't, this is the best I can, Happy Birthday," I say, and set a plate on the table. In the middle of the plate is a jelly sandwich, and in the center of the sandwich is the stub of a lit candle left over from when I was still trying to impress dates. The whole thing looks pretty lame but the girl claps all the same. She tries valiantly to blow the candle out, and then they both try, and after a while they just look up at me, and I do it for them.

I'm not sure what to do next so I ask them if they want to watch Shirley Temple movies, and we go into the living room and sit on the couch and I think they had a good time, though in the morning I discover the jelly sandwich untouched on the plate. It's stale but I eat it just the same, sitting in front of the computer, searching the Internet sites of missing and murdered children, looking for the birthday girl, but I never do find her.

Suddenly it's as if I'm running some kind of day care center for dead kids. She keeps bringing them to me, I don't know why. We watch Shirley Temple movies, though she's the one who likes them best, and, I have to admit, she can be pretty bratty about it at times. Actually, they all can be pretty bratty. They're little kids, what can I say? They fight over which movie to watch, they run up and down the stairs, they jump off the kitchen table and the back of the couch. I recognize some of them. Without asking, I know some of their names. I mean, come on, some of these kids are famous. Others, like the little black girl, I never do figure out. When they're all around, I sometimes think I'm going to lose it, but when no one comes, when it's just me, all alone, staring at the computer again, still trying to find the perfect title, the perfect little phrase to describe what happened to my family, I miss their smelly mouths, their waxy ears, their noise, their demands, their little bodies twisted in odd positions of sleep and play, and I miss their laughter, the gorgeous sound of their laughter. Her dancing. I miss her dancing. And I miss her, most of all.

But she says it's getting boring at my house. She says it's too noisy. She says she might not come around any more and when I ask her to dance she just shakes her head, no; she doesn't feel like it. That's when I say, without thinking about it or anything, why don't we have a party, and she says, "You mean like a jelly sandwich with a candle stuck in it?" (I told you, she can be bratty.) But I say, no, I mean like a big party, with balloons and party hats and paper mache streamers, would you like that? "And a Christmas tree?" she asks. Well, I wasn't really thinking of that but I can tell she wants one so I say sure. She smiles, "And big red Valentine's hearts?" I say, all right, "And Easter Baskets? And chocolate eggs?" And I say sure, of course, it'll be a holiday party, an every holiday party, and I don't say this part, but you know, for all the ones they've missed. She gives me a big hug then, her little arms tight around my neck and she kisses me right on the mouth.

I buy red, green, orange and black streamers, balloons that have "Happy Birthday" printed on them, a paper tablecloth with turkeys and pilgrims on it. I get a seventy-five percent discount on the scarecrow, the ceramic pumpkin, and a clown costume, but I have to pay a ridiculous price for the fake Christmas tree already decorated with lights and ornaments. I buy cupcakes, even though I'm not sure any of the dead kids eat, and I buy two kinds of paper plates, one with Barbie on them, and the other, with Dinosaurs. I get several different kid DVDs (I have to admit even I'm getting a little sick of Shirley Temple) and a CD of Christmas classics.

Sarah Vehler is working again, she is standing there, chewing on a hangnail, and not checking anyone out but I stand in line behind a woman with two little kids, a boy and a girl. The boy is furiously sucking his thumb, and the girl is begging for candy. The woman, their mother, I assume, is ignoring them, paging through a *People* magazine. I smile at the little girl, and for just a second she stops asking for candy and stares at me. Her eyes remind me of beach glass. Sarah Vehler calls my name and when I look up, she waves me over. "Don't you have nothing better to do than stand in line all day?" she says. "Wow, looks like you're planning a full year of parties. How many kids you got anyway?" I shrug, and to change the subject tell her I like her earrings. I have long since learned that the real way to gain a woman's trust is to tell her you like her earrings, but Sarah Vehler just looks at me like I said something crazy and of course that's when I realize she isn't wearing earrings. I laugh, "I mean last time," I say, "I remember the ones you had on last time, and I meant to tell you they were real nice." Then, things only get more ridiculous when she tells me she never wears earrings. "I'm sorry," I say, grabbing the bags and the box of cupcakes. "I thought it was you, but it must have been someone else." She just looks at me like she is thinking real hard, and then she says, "I saw your brother the other day and he says you don't have any kids at all."

I smile, to be polite, and then tilt my chin, like, you got another customer. She turns, and sees the guy who has a disturbingly blank expression on his face, but when she looks at me again, I shrug, as if to say, too bad we can't talk.

When I get home, I have to clean the place. I've let it go and my mother would shit if she saw it, but she never tries to visit, and doesn't even call. She's got her own life now, and doesn't like to be reminded of the old one, I guess, the one me and my brother are stuck in forever. I pick up beer cans and paper plates and realize this hasn't exactly been the best environment for children. I freaking hate to clean, but after a while I sort of get into it, I put one of the new DVDs in, I don't know what it was called but it was bright and noisy and cheerful, it kept me company. I even washed the windows. Then I hung up the streamers, twisting them from the ceiling in the kitchen and the living room, and I set up the tree, and the tablecloth, and the plates, and then I put the clown costume on, and I looked at myself in the mirror, I was wearing a bright red, yellow, blue, and green polka dotted jumpsuit, giant red shoes that flopped six inches from my toes, a bright red wig, and a red nose. I looked at myself for a while, trying to figure out who I reminded myself of, and then I flashed back to a birthday party, was it for me or my brother, my father dressed up like a clown. I grab my phone and call. The answering machine picks up.

"The thing is," I say, "I mean, come on. Don't give up on me so fast, okay? It was just a movie. It's research, all right? Fuck. I mean really, fuck. Look, I didn't give up on you even with all the drugs and the stealing and shit, right? Right?" It seems like I should say something else, something perfect, but I can't think what that would be so I hang up and call Terry.

"The thing is," I say, "I haven't been completely honest."

There's a moment's pause. A long moment before he says, "Shoot."

"The thing is," I say, "what I want to write about isn't an innocent man." I wait, but he doesn't say anything. "The children . . ." She is standing there, in the middle of the living room, staring at the Christmas tree with the strangest expression on her face. She is dressed just like a regular little girl, in little girl pajamas and a bathrobe. I wave at her and point to the phone, signaling that I'll be winding the call up soon, but her expression doesn't change, she looks at me with confusion, and sorrow.

"What about the kids? What's your point? Can you just give it to me in a sentence?"

"The children were telling the truth, my father was not an innocent man."

Terry whistles, long and low. "Fuck," he says.

"You're the first person I ever told."

"Well, this puts us in the crapper without any shit, that's for sure."

"What?" She is reaching for the tree, touching it lightly with her fingertips, as though afraid it will disappear.

"Listen, if that's the case what we got is just another story about a fucking pedophile. Those are a dime a dozen. The market is saturated with them. It's not a special story any more, it's just . . . now wait a second, that kid, you're not saying he had anything to do with that kid's murder are you, 'cause if you were saying that, well then we'd have a story."

"No." She is petting the tree, and this part really gets to me, she leans in to smell it, even though it is fake, she presses her face real close to the branches and then she realizes I am watching and she looks at me again, but in a new way, like she has something she wants to say, like she needs me. "I gotta go," I say.

"I mean even if you think he could have possibly had something to do with it, that we might be able to sell. It gets tricky, 'cause you know all of a sudden everyone's fact checking the hell out of memoirs, but we might be able to work that angle, you know, not that you really believe he killed her, 'cause everyone knows her parents did it, right, but like you could tie her into your story and the idea that your father was someone like her father, you might have something there, okay? We might be able to sell that."

She has big eyes, and they are sad, and she wants to tell me something important, maybe she's going to tell me who did kill her, "Listen, I gotta go," I say. Terry keeps talking, he's getting excited now, just the way, all those years ago, everyone got excited about her murder. I click the phone off.

"What is it?" I say, "You can tell me."

"I wet myself," she says, in the softest little girl voice.

Sure enough, there's a wet stain down the front of her pajamas, and a puddle on the rug beneath the Christmas tree. "That's okay," I say, even as the dank odor reaches me, "sometimes that happens. Why don't you go in the bathroom and take off your clothes. Do you have a way, I mean, I don't know how this works, do you have some clean clothes with you?"

She shakes her head.

I nod, like, okay, no problem. The phone rings and she looks relieved when I don't make any move to answer it. Instead I search through the piles of clothes on my bedroom floor until I find a dingy white T-shirt and a brand new pair of boxer shorts, which of course will be huge on her, so I also give her a tie. She looks up at me with confusion when I hand her the stuff. "It'll be like a costume, for the party. Kind of different from the kind you usually wear, I know. Go in the bathroom, okay, and wash yourself off and take off your wet pajamas and put on the T-shirt, and these shorts, and tie these with this, see, like a belt."

"Will you wipe me?" she says.

I shouldn't be surprised by this; I've read all about how she still asked people to wipe her, even though she was dressed up like a movie star. "No. You have to do it yourself, okay?"

She shakes her head and starts to cry.

One thing I can't stand is a crying kid. "Okay," I say, "okay, just don't cry, all right?"

We walk into the bathroom and I help her out of her pajamas, her skin is white, pure as fresh soap, and she is completely unembarrassed of her nakedness. She smiles when I wipe her, first with toilet paper, and then with a towel dampened with warm water and I just try not to think about anything, about how tiny she is, or how perfect. I help her put the clean T-shirt on and the boxer shorts, which I cinch around her little waist with the tie and by then she is laughing and I am too and we stand before the mirror to look at ourselves but all I see is me, in the ridiculous clown costume. Where does she keep disappearing to? I call her name, searching through all the rooms, thinking she's playing some kind of game, but I can't find her anywhere. The doorbell rings and I run to answer it, laughing because it's very funny the way she's hidden outside but when I open the door, my brother is standing there.

"Oh, fuck," he says.

"It's not the way it looks."

He looks behind me, at the streamers, the table set with Barbie and Dinosaur plates, the cupcakes, the Christmas tree. "Fuck," he says.

"No, wait," I holler, and when he doesn't stop I follow him, flopping down the stairs, "wait," I say, running after him, though it is difficult in the too-big red shoes, the red wig bouncing down my forehead, "it's not how it looks."

He turns, and I smile at him, knowing he'll understand, after all, we share the same childhood, but instead he looks at me with a horrified expression, as if I am a terrifying ghost, and then he turns his back on me and runs. I don't try to follow him; instead I walk back to my house. Someone in a passing car shouts something and throws a paper cup of soda at me, but misses. I am surprised by this, it seems to me clowns deserve a little respect; after all, they only exist to make people laugh.

When I get back inside, I shut the door and sit on the couch in front of the TV and watch the cartoon people, who are shaped like balloons. There are no dead children and there are no secrets in a world where everyone is brightly colored and devoid of the vulnerabilities of flesh. In balloon world all the problems explode or float away. Even though it's been cold and cloudy for weeks, the sun comes out and fills the room with an explosion of light until I can no longer see the picture on the TV screen. One of the streamers comes loose and dangles over my head, twirling, and I can't help but think, that in spite of what Terry said, there is plenty of shit for the crapper, but it doesn't matter, because in the distance, I hear the soft hum of a little girl singing. And just like that my mood improves, because I am waiting for the children, and just thinking about them, makes me smile.

Memoir of a Deer Woman

(New Year's Day)

*H*ER HUSBAND COMES HOME, STAMPS THE SNOW
from his shoes, kisses her, and asks how her day was.

"Our time together is short," she says.

"What are you talking about?"

"I found a deer by the side of the road. It was stuck under the broken fence. Hit by a car. I called the rescue place but when the animal rescue man saw it, he said it had to be shot. The policeman shot it."

He looks through the mail while she stands there, crying. When he realizes this, he hugs her. Already she feels the hard shapes forming at the top of her head. Later, she will tell him she has a headache.

He will hold her anyway. He will sleep with his mouth pressed against her neck. She will think of the noise the deer made, that horrible braying.

At midnight she wakes up. The sky is exploding with distant fireworks. From past experience she knows that if they stand and strain their necks, they can just barely see the veins of color over the treetops. It is mostly futile, and tonight neither of them rises. "Happy New Year," he whispers.

"What do you think animals feel?" she says.

He mumbles something about Wally, their dog, who sleeps soundly at the foot of their bed.

"That deer was frightened. Today, I mean. It made the most horrible noise; did I tell you that? I never heard such a noise before. It was really mournful and horrible."

The fireworks end in a flourish of tiny explosions. She knows what she should have done. She should not have waited for the policeman, who took four shots before he killed it. She knew that deer was dying, why did she pretend otherwise? She should have smothered it and put it out of its misery.

New Year's morning is cold and crisp. Wally wakes them up with his big, wet tongue. Her husband takes him out to do his business. When they come back inside, she listens to the pleasant sounds of her husband talking in soft cooing words to Wally, his food dish being filled. Her husband comes back into the bedroom alone, carefully shutting the door behind him. She knows what that means. He crawls in beside her. He rubs his hands up and down her body. "Happy New Year," he says. She sinks into his desires until they become her own. Who knows how long they have? Maybe this is the last time. Later, he fries maple sausage and scrambles eggs, but she finds she cannot eat. He asks her if she feels all right. She shrugs. "My head hurts," she says. "Also my hands." He tells her to go to the doctor. She nods. Well, of course. But she does not tell him that she already knows what is happening.

She takes down the ornaments, wraps them in tissue paper, circles the tree, removing the lights. The branches brush her cheeks and lips and she nibbles on the bitter green. Her husband is outside, splitting kindling. For a while she stands at the window and watches. Wally lies on his bed in the living room. He does not like the loud noise of the axe. She raises her face to the ceiling. She feels trapped and the feeling rises inside her like bile. She brays. Wally slinks past her, into the kitchen. She brays again. It is both deeply disturbing and a relief.

When her husband comes in, carrying kindling, he'll ask her if she's all right. He'll say he thought he heard a strange noise. She'll shrug and say that she thought the tree was falling. He'll accept this as reasonable, forgetting that she is not the sort to scream at falling Christmas trees, forgetting that when they met she was at least partly wild. He drops the kindling into the box next to the wood-burning stove. "Come here, help me with the tree," she says. He holds the tree while she unscrews the stand. Dry sap snakes from the holes, she cannot help but think of it as blood.

They dump the tree in the forest behind the house. There is a whole graveyard of Christmas trees there. They walk back to the house together, crunching across the snow. A green truck is parked in the driveway. "I wonder who that is," he says. A tall man wearing camouflage clothes and a Crocodile Dundee hat steps out of the driver's side. He nods as they approach.

She knows just what her mother would have said about all of this. She would have said, "You are never going to be tame. You will regret trying. You will hurt others if you deny yourself."

"Hope I'm not disturbing you. I've got an owl that needs to be released. It was found not too far down the road. You know the Paterlys? They're in Florida now. I thought I could release it in your yard. You could keep an eye on it."

"This is Kevin," she tells her husband. "He came to help with the deer yesterday."

Her husband stares at her blankly.

"You know, the one I found? That had to be shot?"

"Can't believe that guy couldn't shoot between the eyes," Kevin says, shaking his head.

"Oh. Right," says her husband.

"Where's the owl?"

"I was just passing by. I'll come back tonight. If that's all right?"

"Tonight?" her husband says.

She tells Kevin that it would be great if he came back later, with the owl. He doesn't look at either of them. He nods at the snow, gets into the truck. They watch him back out of the driveway.

"He's kind of strange," her husband says.

She shrugs. Her bones ache, her head, her hands and her feet, and it takes a lot of effort for her to understand that her husband is not being mean, just human. They walk back to the house, holding hands. Who knows, she thinks, maybe this is the last time. Already by nightfall she is wearing mittens. She tells him her hands are cold. Again he tells her to go to the doctor. She tells him that she has an appointment the next morning. This is love, she reminds herself. She smiles at her husband while he turns the pages of his book.

"Stage three," the doctor says.

"There must be some mistake."

"You can get a second opinion."

"What are my options?"

"I say we hit this with everything we've got."

"Are you sure that's my report?"

"I know this comes as a shock, but I recommend that you address it quickly. The sooner the better."

"Chemo and radiation?"

"Yes. And then chemo again."

"The magic bullets."

"You could think of it that way, but you might want to choose a different image. Something soothing."

"Like what?"

"I have one patient who thinks of the treatment as flowers."

"Flowers?"

"It soothes her."

"What kind of flowers? Flowers that'll cause my hair to fall out and make me throw up? What kind of flowers would do that?"

"This is your disease, and your body. You get to decide how you want to treat it."

"But that's just the thing, isn't it, Doctor?"

"I'm sorry?"

"This isn't my body anymore."

"Why don't you go home? Take the weekend to think about your options? Get a second opinion, if you'd like."

She rises from the chair, stomps out of the office on her sore, hard feet. The waiting room is full of women. One of them looks up, her brown eyes beautiful in the soft pelt of her face. She nods slightly. She smells like salt.

When her husband returns from work she is sitting at the kitchen table, waiting to tell him the news.

"Oh my God," he says.

"It hardly hurts at all."

"How long?" he asks.

"Nobody knows, but it seems to be happening sooner rather than later."

He pounds the table with his fist, then reaches for her hand, though he recoils from the shape. "But you're a woman."

She is confused until she sees where he is looking. She touches the antlers' downy stubs on the top of her head. "It's rare, but females get them too. Nobody knows why. Kind of like men and nipples, I guess."

"What are you going to do?" he asks.

"I'm thinking of writing a memoir."

His mouth drops open.

She shrugs. "I always did want to be a writer."

"What are you talking about?"

"I think I should start with the deer being shot, what do you think?"

"I think you need medicine, not writing."

"You make it sound dirty."

He shakes his head. He is crying and shaking his head and all of a sudden she realizes that he will never understand. Should she say so in her memoir? Should she write about all the places he never understood? Will he understand that she doesn't blame him?

"It isn't lonely," she says.

"What?"

She hadn't meant to speak out loud. "I mean, okay, sometimes it is."

"I don't know what you're talking about."

"There's a memoir-writing group that meets every Wednesday. I e-mailed Anita, the leader? I explained my situation and she was really nice about it. She said I could join them."

"I don't see how this is going to help. You need medicine and doctors. We need to be proactive here."

"Could you just be supportive? I really need your support right now."

He looks at her with teary blue eyes that once, she thought, she would look at forever. He says, his voice husky, "Of course."

She is sniffling, and he wipes her nose for her. She licks his hand.

She continues to sleep with him, but in the morning he wakes up with deep scratch marks all over his body, no matter how thickly they wrap her hooves in layers of cloth and old socks and mittens. "They're like little razors," he says. "And it's not just the edges, it's the entire bottom."

She blinks her large brown eyes at him, but he doesn't notice because he is pulling a tick out of his elbow. That night she sleeps on the floor and Wally crawls into bed with her husband. He objects, of course, but in the end, they both sleep better, she, facing the window where she watches the white owl, hugely fat and round, perched on the bough of a tree, before she realizes it isn't the owl at all but the moon.

*   *   *

Near the end she stops trying to drive; instead she runs to her memoir-writing workshop. Her husband follows in the Volvo, thinking that he can prevent her being hit by a car, or shot. He waits in the driveway while she meets with the group.

Anita tries to make her comfortable, but lately she feels nervous coming all the way into the house. She lies in the doorway with only her nose and front hooves inside. Some of the others complain about the cold and the snow but Anita tells them to put on their coats. Sometimes, in the distance, they hear a mournful cry, which makes all of them shudder. There have been rumors of coyotes in the neighborhood.

Even though they meet at Anita's house, she herself is having a terrible time with her memoir. It sounds self-pitying, whiny, and dull. She knows this; she just doesn't know what to do about it, that's why she started the workshop in the first place. The critiquers mean well, but frankly, they are all self-pitying whiners themselves. Somewhere along the way, the meetings have taken on the tone of group therapy rather than a writing workshop. Yet, there is something, some emotion they all seem to circle but never successfully describe about the pain of their lives that, Anita feels certain, just might be the point.

After the critique, Anita brings out cakes, cookies, coffee, tea, and, incredibly, a salt lick. Contrary to their reputation, and the evidence of the stories told in this room, people can be good.

The deer woman hasn't shared what she's written yet. She's not sure the group will understand. How can anyone understand what is happening to her? And besides, it is all happening so fast. No one even realizes when she attends her last meeting that she won't be coming back, though later, they all agree that she seemed different somehow.

She is standing at the window, watching the yard below. Six deer wait there, staring up at her. He weeps and begs her not to go. Why does he do this, she wonders, why does he spend their last moments together weeping? He begs her not to go, as though she had some say in the matter. She does not answer. The world shatters all around her, but she is not cut. He shouts. She crashes to the ground, in a flurry of snow and hooves. He stands at the window, his mouth wide open. He does not mean to hurt her, but she can feel his breath pulling her back. She runs into the forest with the others, a pounding of hooves and clouds of snow. They do not stop running until they are deep into the night, and she can no longer hear her husband shouting.

After she is gone, he looks through her basket of knitting, projects started and unfinished from the winter, before her hands turned into hooves: a long, thin strand of purple, which he assumes is a scarf; a deep green square, which he thinks might be the beginning of a sweater for him; and a soft, gray wasp nest, that's what it looks like, knit from the strands of her hair. Underneath all this he finds a simple, spiral-bound notebook. He sits on the floor and reads what she wrote, until the words sputter and waver and finally end, then he walks up the stairs to the attic, where he thrusts aside boxes of books, and dolls, cups, and papers, before finally opening the box labeled "writing supplies." There he finds the cape, neatly folded beneath deerskin boots, a few blades of brown grass stuck to them. The cape fits fine, of course, but the boots are too tight. He takes them downstairs and splits the seams with the paring knife, laces them on with rope. When he is finished, he makes a strange sight, his chest hair gray against the winter white skin, the cape draped over his narrow shoulders and down the skein of his arms to his blue jeans, which are tied at the calves, laced over the deerskin, his feet bulging out of the sides, like a child suddenly grown to giant proportions. He runs into the forest, calling her name. Wally, the dog, runs beside him.

There are sightings. An old lady, putting seed into the bird feeder, sees him one morning, a glint of white cape, tight muscles, a wild look in his eyes. Two children, standing right beside their father waiting for the bus, scream and point. An entire group of hunters, who say they tracked him and might have gotten a shot. And an artist, standing in the meadow, but artists are always reporting strange sightings and can't be relied upon. What is certain is that wherever the strange man is sighted, words are found. The old lady finds several tiny slips of paper in a bird nest in her backyard and when one falls to the ground she sees that it is a neat cut-out of the word, "Always," she can't fathom what it might mean, but considers it for the rest of her life, until one afternoon in early autumn she lies dying on her kitchen floor, no trauma beyond the business of a stopped heart, and she sees the word before her face, as though it floated there, a missive from heaven, and she is filled with an understanding of the infinite, and how strange, that this simple word becomes, in that final moment, luminescent; when the father searches the bushes where the children insist the wild man hides, he finds nothing but scraps of paper, tiny pieces, which he almost dismisses, until he realizes that each one contains a word. Frightened of leaving the children too long with madmen about, he scoops some words up and returns to the bus stop, listening to the children's excited chatter but not really hearing anything they say, because the words drag his pocket down like stones, and he can't believe how eager he is to go to work, shut the door to his office and piece together the meaning. He is disappointed at what he finds, "breath," "fingers," and "memory," amongst several versions of "her." It is nonsense, but he cannot forget the words, and at the strangest times catches himself thinking, "Her breath, her fingers, her memory" as though he were a man in love; the hunters follow the trail of words, but only the youngest among them picks up and pockets one torn paper, which is immediately forgotten, thrown in the wash and destroyed; the artist finds a neat little pile, as though the wild creature ate words like sunflower seeds and left these scraps behind. She ties each word to colored string and hangs them as a mobile. Sometimes, when the air is just right and the words spin gently, she believes she understands them, that they are not simple nonsense; but on other days she knows that meaning is something humans apply to random acts in order to cope with the randomness of death.

Anita, from the memoir-writing group, goes to the house, uninvited. She doesn't know what motivates her. The woman wrote nothing the whole time she'd attended, had offered no suggestions during the critique; in fact, Anita began to suspect that her main motivation for coming had been the salt lick. But for some reason, Anita felt invested in the woman's unknown story, and feels she must find out what has become of her.

What she finds is a small house in the woods, by all appearances empty. She rings the doorbell and is surprised to hear a dog inside, barking. She notices deer tracks come right up to the porch, circling a hemlock bush. The door opens and a strange man stands there, dressed in torn boots, dirty jeans, and a cape. Anita has heard rumors of the wild man and doesn't know what to say, she manages only two words, "Memoir" and "writing," before he grabs her wrist. "Gone," he says, "gone." They stand there for a while, looking at each other. She is a bit frightened, of course, but she also feels pity for this man, obviously mad with grief. "Words?" he says. She stares at him, and he repeats himself, ("Words, words, words, words, words, words?") until finally she understands what he's asking.

"She never wrote a thing." He shakes his head and runs back into the house. Anita stands there for a moment, and then, just as she turns to walk away from this tragic scene, the man returns, carrying a handful of words. He hands them to her as though they were ashes of the deceased, gently folding her fingers over them, as though in prayer, before he goes back inside.

She shakes her head as she walks away, opening the car door with difficulty, her hands fisted as they are. Once in her car, she drops the words into her purse, where they remain until a windy day in early fall, when she searches for her keys in the mall parking lot. A quick breeze picks the tiny scraps up and they twirl in the sky, all the possible, all the forgotten, all the mysterious, unwritten, and misunderstood fragments, and it is only then, when they are hopelessly gone, that Anita regrets having done nothing with them. From this regret, her memoir is written, about the terrible thing that happened to her. She is finally able to write that there is no sorrow greater than regret, no rapture more complete than despair, no beauty more divine than words, but before writing it, she understands, standing there, amidst the cars and shopping bags, watching all the words spin away, as though she had already died, and no longer owned language, that ordinary, everyday, exquisite blessing on which lives are both built, and destroyed.

Journey into the Kingdom

(Valentine's Day)

THE FIRST PAINTING WAS OF AN EGG, THE PALE ovoid produced with faint strokes of pink, blue, and violet to create the illusion of white. After that there were two apples, a pear, an avocado, and finally, an empty plate on a white tablecloth before a window covered with gauzy curtains, a single fly nestled in a fold at the top right corner. The series was titled "Journey into the Kingdom." On a small table beneath the avocado there was a black binder, an unevenly cut rectangle of white paper with the words "Artist's Statement" in neat, square, hand-written letters taped to the front. Balancing the porcelain cup and saucer with one hand, Alex picked up the binder and took it with him to a small table against the wall toward the back of the coffee shop, where he opened it, thinking it might be interesting to read something besides the newspaper for once, though he almost abandoned the idea when he saw that the page before him was handwritten in the same neat letters as on the cover. But the title intrigued him.

AN IMITATION LIFE

Though I always enjoyed my crayons and watercolors, I was not a particularly artistic child. I produced the usual assortment of stick figures and houses with dripping yellow suns. I was an avid collector of seashells and sea glass and much preferred to be outdoors, throwing stones at seagulls (please, no haranguing from animal rights activists, I have long since outgrown this) or playing with my imaginary friends to sitting quietly in the salt rooms of the keeper's house, making pictures at the big wooden kitchen table while my mother, in her black dress, kneaded bread and sang the old French songs between her duties as lighthouse keeper, watcher over the waves, beacon for the lost, governess of the dead.

The first ghost to come to my mother was my own father who had set out the day previous in the small boat heading to the mainland for supplies such as string and rice, and also bags of soil, which, in years past, we emptied into crevices between the rocks and planted with seeds, a makeshift garden and a "brave attempt," as my father called it, referring to the barren stone we lived on.

We did not expect him for several days so my mother was surprised when he returned in a storm, dripping wet icicles from his mustache and behaving strangely, repeating over and over again, "It is lost, my dear Maggie, the garden is at the bottom of the sea."

My mother fixed him hot tea but he refused it, she begged him to take off the wet clothes and retire with her, to their feather bed piled with quilts, but he said, "Tend the light, don't waste your time with me." So my mother, a worried expression on her face, left our little keeper's house and walked against the gale to the lighthouse, not realizing that she left me with a ghost, melting before the fire into a great puddle, which was all that was left of him upon her return. She searched frantically while I kept pointing at the puddle and insisting it was he. Eventually she tied on her cape and went out into the storm, calling his name. I thought that, surely, I would become orphaned that night.

But my mother lived, though she took to her bed and left me to tend the lamp and receive the news of the discovery of my father's wrecked boat, found on the rocky shoals, still clutching in his frozen hand a bag of soil, which was given to me, and which I brought to my mother though she would not take the offering.

For one so young, my chores were immense. I tended the lamp, and kept our own hearth fire going too. I made broth and tea for my mother, which she only gradually took, and I planted that small bag of soil by the door to our little house, savoring the rich scent, wondering if those who lived with it all the time appreciated its perfume or not.

I did not really expect anything to grow, though I hoped that the seagulls might drop some seeds or the ocean deposit some small thing. I was surprised when, only weeks later, I discovered the tiniest shoots of green, which I told my mother about. She was not impressed. By that point, she would spend part of the day sitting up in bed, mending my father's socks and moaning, "Agatha, whatever are we going to do?" I did not wish to worry her, so I told her lies about women from the mainland coming to help, men taking turns with the light. "But they are so quiet. I never hear anyone."

"No one wants to disturb you," I said. "They whisper and walk on tiptoe."

It was only when I opened the keeper's door so many uncounted weeks later, and saw, spread before me, embedded throughout the rock (even in crevices where I had planted no soil) tiny pink, purple, and white flowers, their stems shuddering in the salty wind, that I insisted my mother get out of bed.

She was resistant at first. But I begged and cajoled, promised her it would be worth her effort. "The fairies have planted flowers for us," I said, this being the only explanation or description I could think of for the infinitesimal blossoms everywhere.

Reluctantly, she followed me through the small living room and kitchen, observing that, "the ladies have done a fairly good job of keeping the place neat." She hesitated before the open door. The bright sun and salty scent of the sea, as well as the loud sound of waves washing all around us, seemed to astound her, but then she squinted, glanced at me, and stepped through the door to observe the miracle of the fairies' flowers.

Never had the rock seen such color, never had it known such bloom! My mother walked out, barefoot, and said, "Forget-me-nots, these are forget-me-nots. But where . . . ?"

I told her that I didn't understand it myself, how I had planted the small bag of soil found clutched in my father's hand but had not really expected it to come to much, and certainly not to all of this, waving my arm over the expanse, the flowers having grown in soil-less crevices and cracks, covering our entire little island of stone.

My mother turned to me and said, "These are not from the fairies, they are from him." Then she started crying, a reaction I had not expected and tried to talk her out of, but she said, "No, Agatha, leave me alone."

She stood out there for quite a while, weeping as she walked amongst the flowers. Later, after she came inside and said, "Where are all the helpers today?" I shrugged and avoided more questions by going outside myself, where I discovered scarlet spots amongst the bloom. My mother had been bedridden for so long, her feet had gone soft again. For days she left tiny teardrop shapes of blood in her step, which I surreptitiously wiped up, not wanting to draw any attention to the fact, for fear it would dismay her. She picked several of the forget-me-not blossoms and pressed them between the heavy pages of her book of myths and folklore. Not long after that, a terrible storm blew in, rocking our little house, challenging our resolve, and taking with it all the flowers. Once again our rock was barren. I worried what effect this would have on my mother but she merely sighed, shrugged, and said, "They were beautiful, weren't they, Agatha?"

So passed my childhood: a great deal of solitude, the occasional life-threatening adventure, the drudgery of work, and all around me the great wide sea with its myriad secrets and reasons, the lost we saved, those we didn't. And the ghosts, brought to us by my father, though we never understood clearly his purpose, as they only stood before the fire, dripping and melting like something made of wax, bemoaning what was lost (a fine boat, a lady love, a dream of the sea, a pocketful of jewels, a wife and children, a carving on bone, a song, its lyrics forgotten). We tried to provide what comfort we could, listening, nodding, there was little else we could do, they refused tea or blankets, they seemed only to want to stand by the fire, mourning their death, as my father stood sentry beside them, melting into salty puddles that we mopped up with clean rags, wrung out into the ocean, saying what we fashioned as prayer, or reciting lines of Irish poetry.

Though I know now that this is not a usual childhood, it was usual for me, and it did not veer from this course until my mother's hair had gone quite gray and I was a young woman, when my father brought us a different sort of ghost entirely, a handsome young man, his eyes the same blue-green as summer. His hair was of indeterminate color, wet curls that hung to his shoulders. Dressed simply, like any dead sailor, he carried about him an air of being educated more by art than by water, a suspicion soon confirmed for me when he refused an offering of tea by saying, "No, I will not, cannot drink your liquid offered without first asking for a kiss, ah a kiss is all the liquid I desire, come succor me with your lips."

Naturally, I blushed and, just as naturally, when my mother went to check on the lamp, and my father had melted into a mustached puddle, I kissed him. Though I should have been warned by the icy chill, as certainly I should have been warned by the fact of my own father, a mere puddle at the hearth, it was my first kiss and it did not feel deadly to me at all, not dangerous, not spectral, most certainly not spectral, though I did experience a certain pleasant floating sensation in its wake.

My mother was surprised, upon her return, to find the lad still standing, as vigorous as any living man, beside my father's puddle. We were both surprised that he remained throughout the night, regaling us with stories of the wild sea populated by whales, mermaids, and sharks; mesmerizing us with descriptions of the "bottom of the world" as he called it, embedded with strange purple rocks, pink shells spewing pearls, and the seaweed tendrils of sea witches' hair. We were both surprised that, when the black of night turned to the gray hue of morning, he bowed to each of us (turned fully toward me, so that I could receive his wink), promised he would return, and then left, walking out the door like any regular fellow. So convincing was he that my mother and I opened the door to see where he had gone, scanning the rock and the inky sea before we accepted that, as odd as it seemed, as vigorous his demeanor, he was a ghost most certainly.

"Or something of that nature," said my mother. "Strange that he didn't melt like the others." She squinted at me and I turned away from her before she could see my blush. "We shouldn't have let him keep us up all night," she said. "We aren't dead. We need our sleep."

Sleep? Sleep? I could not sleep, feeling as I did his cool lips on mine, the power of his kiss, as though he breathed out of me some dark aspect that had weighed inside me. I told my mother that she could sleep. I would take care of everything. She protested, but using the past as reassurance (she had long since discovered that I had run the place while she convalesced after my father's death), finally agreed.

I was happy to have her tucked safely in bed. I was happy to know that her curious eyes were closed. I did all the tasks necessary to keep the place in good order. Not even then, in all my girlish giddiness, did I forget the lamp. I am embarrassed to admit, however, it was well past four o'clock before I remembered my father's puddle, which by that time had been much dissipated. I wiped up the small amount of water and wrung him out over the sea, saying only as prayer, "Father, forgive me. Oh, bring him back to me." (Meaning, alas for me, a foolish girl, the boy who kissed me and not my own dear father.)

And that night, he did come back, knocking on the door like any living man, carrying in his wet hands a bouquet of pink coral, which he presented to me, and a small white stone, shaped like a star, which he gave to my mother.

"Is there no one else with you?" she asked.

"I'm sorry, there is not," he said.

My mother began to busy herself in the kitchen, leaving the two of us alone. I could hear her in there, moving things about, opening cupboards, sweeping the already swept floor. It was my own carelessness that had caused my father's absence, I was sure of that; had I sponged him up sooner, had I prayed for him more sincerely, and not just for the satisfaction of my own desire, he would be here this night. I felt terrible about this, but then I looked into his eyes, those beautiful sea-colored eyes, and I could not help it, my body thrilled at his look. Is this love? I thought. Will he kiss me twice? When it seemed as if, without even wasting time with words, he was about to do so, leaning toward me with parted lips from which exhaled the scent of salt water, my mother stepped into the room, clearing her throat, holding the broom before her, as if thinking she might use it as a weapon.

"We don't really know anything about you," she said.

To begin with, my name is Ezekiel. My mother was fond of saints and the Bible and such. She died shortly after giving birth to me, her first and only child. I was raised by my father, on the island of Murano. Perhaps you have heard of it? Murano glass? We are famous for it throughout the world. My father, himself, was a talented glassmaker. Anything imagined, he could shape into glass. Glass birds, tiny glass bees, glass seashells, even glass tears (an art he perfected while I was an infant), and what my father knew, he taught to me.

Naturally, I eventually surpassed him in skill. Forgive me, but there is no humble way to say it. At any rate, my father had taught me and encouraged my talent all my life. I did not see when his enthusiasm began to sour. I was excited and pleased at what I could produce. I thought he would feel the same for me as I had felt for him, when, as a child, I sat on the footstool in his studio and applauded each glass wing, each hard teardrop.

Alas, it was not to be. My father grew jealous of me. My own father! At night he snuck into our studio and broke my birds, my little glass cakes. In the morning he pretended dismay and instructed me further on keeping air bubbles out of my work. He did not guess that I knew the dismal truth.

I determined to leave him, to sail away to some other place to make my home. My father begged me to stay, "Whatever will you do? How will you make your way in this world?"

I told him my true intention, not being clever enough to lie. "This is not the only place in the world with fire and sand," I said. "I intend to make glass."

He promised me it would be a death sentence. At the time I took this to be only his confused, fatherly concern. I did not perceive it as a threat.

It is true that the secret to glassmaking was meant to remain on Murano. It is true that the entire populace believed this trade, and only this trade, kept them fed and clothed. Finally, it is true that they passed the law (many years before my father confronted me with it) that anyone who dared attempt to take the secret of glassmaking off the island would suffer the penalty of death. All of this is true.

But what's also true is that I was a prisoner in my own home, tortured by my own father, who pretended to be a humble, kind glassmaker, but who, night after night, broke my creations and then, each morning, denied my accusations, his sweet, old face mustached and whiskered, all the expression of dismay and sorrow.

This is madness, I reasoned. How else could I survive? One of us had to leave or die. I chose the gentler course.

We had, in our possession, only a small boat, used for trips that never veered far from shore. Gathering mussels, visiting neighbors, occasionally my father liked to sit in it and smoke a pipe while watching the sun set. He'd light a lantern and come home, smelling of the sea, boil us a pot of soup, a melancholic, completely innocent air about him, only later to sneak about his breaking work.

This small boat is what I took for my voyage across the sea. I also took some fishing supplies, a rope, dried cod he'd stored for winter, a blanket, and several jugs of red wine, given to us by the baker, whose daughter, I do believe, fancied me. For you, who have lived so long on this anchored rock, my folly must be apparent. Was it folly? It was. But what else was I to do? Day after day I make my perfect art only to have my father, night after night, destroy it? He would destroy me!

I left in the dark, when the ocean is like ink and the sky is black glass with thousands of air bubbles. Air bubbles, indeed. I breathed my freedom in the salty sea air. I chose stars to follow. Foolishly, I had no clear sense of my passage and had only planned my escape.

Of course, knowing what I do now about the ocean, it is a wonder I survived the first night, much less seven. It was on the eighth morning that I saw the distant sail, and, hopelessly drunk and sunburned, as well as lost, began the desperate task of rowing toward it, another folly as I'm sure you'd agree, understanding how distant the horizon is. Luckily for me, or so I thought, the ship headed in my direction and after a few more days it was close enough that I began to believe in my life again.

Alas, this ship was owned by a rich friend of my father's, a woman who had commissioned him to create a glass castle with a glass garden and glass fountain, tiny glass swans, a glass king and queen, a baby glass princess, and glass trees with golden glass apples, all for the amusement of her granddaughter (who, it must be said, had fingers like sausages and broke half of the figurines before her next birthday). This silly woman was only too happy to let my father use her ship, she was only too pleased to pay the ship's crew, all with the air of helping my father, when, in truth, it simply amused her to be involved in such drama. She said she did it for Murano, but in truth, she did it for the story.

It wasn't until I had been rescued, and hoisted on board, that my father revealed himself to me. He spread his arms wide, all great show for the crew, hugged me and even wept, but convincing as was his act, I knew he intended to destroy me.

These are terrible choices no son should have to make, but that night, as my father slept and the ship rocked its weary way back to Murano where I would likely be hung or possibly sentenced to live with my own enemy, my father, I slit the old man's throat. Though he opened his eyes, I do not believe he saw me, but was already entering the distant kingdom.

You ladies look quite aghast. I cannot blame you. Perhaps I should have chosen my own death instead, but I was a young man, and I wanted to live. Even after everything I had gone through, I wanted life.

Alas, it was not to be. I knew there would be trouble and accusation if my father were found with his throat slit, but none at all if he just disappeared in the night, as so often happens on large ships. Many a traveler has simply fallen overboard, never to be heard from again, and my father had already displayed a lack of seafaring savvy to rival my own.

I wrapped him up in the now-bloody blanket but although he was a small man, the effect was still that of a body, so I realized I would have to bend and fold him into a rucksack. You wince, but do not worry, he was certainly dead by this time.

I will not bore you with the details of my passage, hiding and sneaking with my dismal load. Suffice it to say that it took a while for me to at last be standing shipside, and I thought then that all danger had passed.

Remember, I was already quite weakened by my days adrift, and the matter of taking care of this business with my father had only fatigued me further. Certain that I was finally at the end of my task, I grew careless. He was much heavier than he had ever appeared to be. It took all my strength to hoist the rucksack, and (to get the sad, pitiable truth over with as quickly as possible) when I heaved that rucksack, the cord became entangled on my wrist, and yes, dear ladies, I went over with it, to the bottom of the world. There I remained until your own dear father, your husband, found me and brought me to this place, where, for the first time in my life, I feel safe, and, though I am dead, blessed.

Later, after my mother had tended the lamp while Ezekiel and I shared the kisses that left me breathless, she asked him to leave, saying that I needed my sleep. I protested, of course, but she insisted. I walked my ghost to the door, just as I think any girl would do in a similar situation, and there, for the first time, he kissed me in full view of my mother, not so passionate as those kisses that had preceded it, but effective nonetheless.

But after he was gone, even as I still blushed, my mother spoke in a grim voice, "Don't encourage him, Agatha."

"Why?" I asked, my body trembling with the impact of his affection and my mother's scorn, as though the two emotions met in me and quaked there. "What don't you like about him?"

"He's dead," she said, "there's that for a start."

"What about Daddy? He's dead too, and you've been loving him all this time."

My mother shook her head. "Agatha, it isn't the same thing. Think about what this boy told you tonight. He murdered his own father."

"I can't believe you'd use that against him. You heard what he said. He was just defending himself."

"But Agatha, it isn't what's said that is always the most telling. Don't you know that? Have I really raised you to be so gullible?"

"I am not gullible. I'm in love."

"I forbid it."

Certainly no three words, spoken by a parent, can do more to solidify love than these. It was no use arguing. What would be the point? She, this woman who had loved no one but a puddle for so long, could never understand what was going through my heart. Without more argument, I went to bed, though I slept fitfully, feeling torn from my life in every way, while my mother stayed up reading, I later surmised, from her book of myths. In the morning I found her sitting at the kitchen table, the great volume before her. She looked up at me with dark circled eyes, then, without salutation, began reading, her voice, ominous.

"There are many kinds of ghosts. There are the ghosts that move things, slam doors and drawers, throw silverware about the house. There are the ghosts (usually of small children) that play in dark corners with spools of thread and frighten family pets. There are the weeping and wailing ghosts. There are the ghosts who know that they are dead, and those who do not. There are tree ghosts, those who spend their afterlife in a particular tree (a clue for such a resident might be bite marks on fallen fruit). There are ghosts trapped forever at the hour of their death (I saw one like this once, in an old movie theater bathroom, hanging from the ceiling). There are melting ghosts (we know about these, don't we?), usually victims of drowning. And there are breath-stealing ghosts. These, sometimes mistaken for the grosser vampire, sustain a sort of half-life by stealing breath from the living. They can be any age, but are usually teenagers and young adults, often at that selfish stage when they died. These ghosts greedily go about sucking the breath out of the living. This can be done by swallowing the lingered breath from unwashed cups, or, most effectively of all, through a kiss. Though these ghosts can often be quite seductively charming, they are some of the most dangerous. Each life has only a certain amount of breath within it and these ghosts are said to steal a finite amount with each swallow. The effect is such that the ghost, while it never lives again, begins to do a fairly good imitation of life, while its victims (those whose breath it steals) edge ever closer to their own death."

My mother looked up at me triumphantly and I stormed out of the house, only to be confronted with the sea all around me, as desolate as my heart.

That night, when he came, knocking on the door, she did not answer it and forbade me to do so.

"It doesn't matter," I taunted, "he's a ghost. He doesn't need doors."

"No, you're wrong," she said, "he's taken so much of your breath that he's not entirely spectral. He can't move through walls any longer. He needs you, but he doesn't care about you at all, don't you get that, Agatha?"

"Agatha? Are you home? Agatha? Why don't you come? Agatha?"

I couldn't bear it. I began to weep.

"I know this is hard," my mother said, "but it must be done. Listen, his voice is already growing faint. We just have to get through this night."

"What about the lamp?" I said.

"What?"

But she knew what I meant. Her expression betrayed her. "Don't you need to check on the lamp?"

"Agatha? Have I done something wrong?"

My mother stared at the door, and then turned to me, the dark circles under her eyes giving her the look of a beaten woman. "The lamp is fine."

I spun on my heels and went into my small room, slammed the door behind me. My mother, a smart woman, was not used to thinking like a warden. She had forgotten about my window. By the time I hoisted myself down from it, Ezekiel was standing on the rocky shore, surveying the dark ocean before him. He had already lost some of his life-like luster, particularly below his knees where I could almost see through him. "Ezekiel," I said. He turned and I gasped at the change in his visage, the cavernous look of his eyes, the skeletal stretch at his jaw. Seeing my shocked expression, he nodded and spread his arms open, as if to say, yes, this is what has become of me. I ran into those open arms and embraced him, though he creaked like something made of old wood. He bent down, pressing his cold lips against mine until they were no longer cold but burning like a fire.

We spent that night together and I did not mind the shattering wind with its salt bite on my skin, and I did not care when the lamp went out and the sea roiled beneath a black sky, and I did not worry about the dead weeping on the rocky shore, or the lightness I felt as though I were floating beside my lover, and when morning came, revealing the dead all around us, I followed him into the water, I followed him to the bottom of the sea, where he turned to me and said,

"What have you done? Are you stupid? Don't you realize? You're no good to me dead!"

So, sadly, like many a daughter, I learned that my mother had been right after all, and when I returned to her, dripping with salt-water and seaweed, tiny fish corpses dropping from my hair, she embraced me. Seeing my state, weeping, she kissed me on the lips, our mouths open. I drank from her, sweet breath, until I was filled and she collapsed to the floor, my mother in her black dress, like a crushed funeral flower.

I had no time for mourning. The lamp had been out for hours. Ships had crashed and men had died. Outside the sun sparkled on the sea. People would be coming soon to find out what had happened.

I took our small boat and rowed away from there. Many hours later, I docked in a seaside town and hitchhiked to another, until eventually I was as far from my home as I could be and still be near my ocean.

I had a difficult time of it for a while. People are generally suspicious of someone with no past and little future. I lived on the street and had to beg for jobs cleaning toilets and scrubbing floors, only through time and reputation working up to my current situation, finally getting my own little apartment, small and dark, so different from when I was the lighthouse keeper's daughter and the ocean was my yard.

One day, after having passed it for months without a thought, I went into the art supply store, and bought a canvas, paint, and two paintbrushes. I paid for it with my tip money, counting it out for the clerk whose expression suggested I was placing turds in her palm instead of pennies. I went home and hammered a nail into the wall, hung the canvas on it, and began to paint. Like many a creative person I seem to have found some solace for the unfortunate happenings of my young life (and death) in art.

I live simply and virginally, never taking breath through a kiss. This is the vow I made, and I have kept it. Yes, some days I am weakened, and tempted to restore my vigor with such an easy solution, but instead I hold the empty cups to my face, I breathe in, I breathe everything, the breath of old men, breath of young, sweet breath, sour breath, breath of lipstick, breath of smoke. It is not, really, a way to live, but this is not, really, a life.

For several seconds after Alex finished reading the remarkable account, his gaze remained transfixed on the page. Finally, he looked up, blinked in the dim coffee shop light, and closed the black binder.

Several baristas stood behind the counter busily jostling around each other with porcelain cups, teapots, bags of beans. One of them, a short girl with red and green hair that spiked around her like some otherworld halo, stood by the sink, stacking dirty plates and cups. When she saw him watching, she smiled. It wasn't a true smile, not that it was mocking, but rather, the girl with the Christmas hair smiled like someone who had either forgotten happiness entirely, or never known it at all. In response, Alex nodded at her, and to his surprise, she came over, carrying a dirty rag and a spray bottle.

"Did you read all of it?" she said as she squirted the table beside him and began to wipe it with the dingy towel.

Alex winced at the unpleasant odor of the cleaning fluid, nodded, and then, seeing that the girl wasn't really paying any attention, said, "Yes." He glanced at the wall where the paintings were hung. "So what'd you think?"

The girl stood there, grinning that sad grin, right next to him now with her noxious bottle and dirty rag, one hip jutted out in a way he found oddly sexual. He opened his mouth to speak, gestured toward the paintings, and then at the book before him. "I, I have to meet her," he said, tapping the book, "this is remarkable."

"But what do you think about the paintings?"

Once more he glanced at the wall where they hung. He shook his head, "No," he said, "it's this," tapping the book again.

She smiled, a true smile, cocked her head, and put out her hand, "Agatha," she said.

Alex felt like his head was spinning. He shook the girl's hand. It was unexpectedly tiny, like that of a child's, and he gripped it too tightly at first. Glancing at the counter, she pulled out a chair and sat down in front of him.

"I can only talk for a little while. Marnie is the manager today and she's on the rag or something all the time, but she's downstairs right now, checking in an order."

"You," he brushed the binder with the tip of his fingers, as if caressing something holy, "you wrote this?"

She nodded, bowed her head slightly, shrugged, and suddenly earnest, leaned across the table, elbowing his empty cup as she did. "Nobody bothers to read it. I've seen a few people pick it up but you're the first one to read the whole thing."

Alex leaned back, frowning.

She rolled her eyes, which, he noticed, were a lovely shade of lavender, lined darkly in black.

"See, I was trying to do something different. This is the whole point," she jabbed at the book, and he felt immediately protective of it, "I was trying to put a story in a place where people don't usually expect one. Don't you think we've gotten awful complacent in our society about story? Like it all the time has to go a certain way and even be only in certain places. That's what this is all about. The paintings are a foil. But you get that, don't you? Do you know," she leaned so close to him, he could smell her breath, which he thought was strangely sweet, "someone actually offered to buy the fly painting?" Her mouth dropped open, she shook her head and rolled those lovely lavender eyes. "I mean, what the fuck? Doesn't he know it sucks?"

Alex wasn't sure what to do. She seemed to be leaning near to his cup. Leaning over it, Alex realized. He opened his mouth, not having any idea what to say.

Just then another barista, the one who wore scarves all the time and had an imperious air about her, as though she didn't really belong there but was doing research or something, walked past. Agatha glanced at her. "I gotta go." She stood up. "You finished with this?" she asked, touching his cup.

Though he hadn't yet had his free refill, Alex nodded.

"It was nice talking to you," she said. "Just goes to show, doesn't it?"

Alex had no idea what she was talking about. He nodded half-heartedly, hoping comprehension would follow, but when it didn't, he raised his eyebrows at her instead.

She laughed. "I mean you don't look anything like the kind of person who would understand my stuff."

"Well, you don't look much like Agatha," he said.

"But I am Agatha," she murmured as she turned away from him, picking up an empty cup and saucer from a nearby table.

Alex watched her walk to the tiny sink at the end of the counter. She set the cups and saucers down. She rinsed the saucers and placed them in the gray bucket they used for carrying dirty dishes to the back. She reached for a cup, and then looked at him.

He quickly looked down at the black binder, picked it up, pushed his chair in, and headed toward the front of the shop. He stopped to look at the paintings. They were fine, boring, but fine little paintings that had no connection to what he'd read. He didn't linger over them for long. He was almost to the door when she was beside him, saying, "I'll take that." He couldn't even fake innocence. He shrugged and handed her the binder.

"I'm flattered, really," she said. But she didn't try to continue the conversation. She set the book down on the table beneath the painting of the avocado. He watched her pick up an empty cup and bring it toward her face, breathing in the lingered breath that remained. She looked up suddenly, caught him watching, frowned, and turned away.

Alex understood. She wasn't what he'd been expecting either. But when love arrives it doesn't always appear as expected. He couldn't just ignore it. He couldn't pretend it hadn't happened. He walked out of the coffee shop into the afternoon sunshine.

Of course, there were problems, her not being alive for one. But Alex was not a man of prejudice.

He was patient besides. He stood in the art supply store for hours, pretending particular interest in the anatomical hinged figurines of sexless men and women in the front window, before she walked past, her hair glowing like a forest fire.

"Agatha," he called.

She turned, frowned, and continued walking. He had to take little running steps to catch up. "Hi," he said. He saw that she was biting her lower lip. "You just getting off work?"

She stopped walking right in front of the bank, which was closed by then, and squinted up at him.

"Alex," he said. "I was talking to you today at the coffee shop."

"I know who you are."

Her tone was angry. He couldn't understand it. Had he insulted her somehow?

"I don't have Alzheimer's. I remember you."

He nodded. This was harder than he had expected.

"What do you want?" she said.

Her tone was really downright hostile. He shrugged. "I just thought we could, you know, talk."

She shook her head. "Listen, I'm happy that you liked my story."

"I did," he said, nodding, "it was great."

"But what would we talk about? You and me?"

Alex shifted beneath her lavender gaze. He licked his lips. She wasn't even looking at him, but glancing around him and across the

street. "I don't care if it does mean I'll die sooner," he said. "I want
to give you a kiss."

Her mouth dropped open.

"Is something wrong?"

She turned and ran. She wore one red sneaker and one green.
They matched her hair.

As Alex walked back to his car, parked in front of the coffee shop,
he tried to talk himself into not feeling so bad about the way things
went. He hadn't always been like this. He used to be able to talk to
people. Even women. Okay, he had never been suave, he knew that,
but he'd been a regular guy. Certainly no one had ever run away
from him before. But after Tessie died, people changed. Of course,
this made sense, initially. He was in mourning, even if he didn't
cry (something the doctor told him not to worry about because one
day, probably when he least expected it, the tears would fall). He
was obviously in pain. People were very nice. They talked to him in
hushed tones. Touched him, gently. Even men tapped him with
their fingertips. All this gentle touching had been augmented by vigorous hugs. People either touched him as if he would break, or
hugged him as if he had already broken and only the vigor of the
embrace kept him intact.

For the longest time there had been all this activity around him.
People called, sent chatty e-mails, even handwritten letters, cards
with flowers on them and prayers. People brought over casseroles,
and bread, Jell-O with fruit in it. (Nobody brought chocolate chip
cookies, which he might have actually eaten.)

To Alex's surprise, once Tessie had died, it felt as though a great
weight had been lifted from him, but instead of appreciating the
feeling, the freedom of being lightened of the burden of his wife's
dying body, he felt in danger of floating away or disappearing. Could
it be possible, he wondered, that Tessie's body, even when she was
mostly bones and barely breath, was all that kept him real? Was it
possible that he would have to live like this, held to life by some
strange force but never a part of it again? These questions led Alex to
the brief period where he'd experimented with becoming a Hare
Krishna, shaved his head, dressed in orange robes, and took up
dancing in the park. Alex wasn't sure but he thought that was when
people started treating him as if he were strange, and even after he
grew his hair out and started wearing regular clothes again, people
continued to treat him strangely.

And, Alex had to admit, as he inserted his key into the lock of his car, he'd forgotten how to behave. How to be normal, he guessed.

You just don't go read something somebody wrote and decide you love her, he scolded himself as he eased into traffic. You don't just go falling in love with breath-stealing ghosts. People don't do that.

Alex did not go to the coffee shop the next day, or the day after that, but it was the only coffee shop in town, and had the best coffee in the state. They roasted the beans right there. Freshness like that can't be faked.

It was awkward for him to see her behind the counter, over by the dirty cups, of course. But when she looked up at him, he attempted a kind smile, then looked away.

He wasn't there to bother her. He ordered French Roast in a cup to go, even though he hated to drink out of paper, paid for it, dropped the change into the tip jar, and left without any further interaction with her.

He walked to the park, where he sat on a bench and watched a woman with two small boys feed white bread to the ducks. This was illegal because the ducks would eat all the bread offered to them, they had no sense of appetite, or being full, and they would eat until their stomachs exploded. Or something like that. Alex couldn't exactly remember. He was pretty sure it killed them. But Alex couldn't decide what to do. Should he go tell that lady and those two little boys that they were killing the ducks? How would that make them feel, especially as they were now triumphantly shaking out the empty bag, the ducks crowded around them, one of the boys squealing with delight? Maybe he should just tell her, quietly. But she looked so happy. Maybe she'd been having a hard time of it. He saw those mothers on *Oprah*, saying what a hard job it was, and maybe she'd had that kind of morning, even screaming at the kids, and then she got this idea, to take them to the park and feed the ducks and now she felt good about what she'd done and maybe she was thinking that she wasn't such a bad mom after all, and if Alex told her she was killing the ducks, would it stop the ducks from dying or just stop her from feeling happiness? Alex sighed. He couldn't decide what to do. The ducks were happy, the lady was happy, and one of the boys was happy. The other one looked sort of terrified. She picked him up and they walked away together, she, carrying the boy who waved the empty bag like a balloon, the other one skipping after them, a few ducks hobbling behind.

For three days Alex ordered his coffee to go and drank it in the park. On the fourth day, Agatha wasn't anywhere that he could see and he surmised that it was her day off so he sat at his favorite table in the back. But on the fifth day, even though he didn't see her again, and it made sense that she'd have two days off in a row, he ordered his coffee to go and took it to the park. He'd grown to like sitting on the bench watching strolling park visitors, the running children, the dangerously fat ducks.

He had no idea she would be there and he felt himself blush when he saw her coming down the path that passed right in front of him. He stared deeply into his cup and fought the compulsion to run. He couldn't help it, though. Just as the toes of her red and green sneakers came into view he looked up. I'm not going to hurt you, he thought, and then, he smiled, that false smile he'd been practicing on her and, incredibly, she smiled back! Also, falsely, he assumed, but he couldn't blame her for that.

She looked down the path and he followed her gaze, seeing that, though the path around the duck pond was lined with benches every fifty feet or so, all of them were taken. She sighed. "Mind if I sit here?"

He scooted over and she sat down, slowly. He glanced at her profile. She looked worn out, he decided. Her lavender eye flickered toward him, and he looked into his cup again. It made sense that she would be tired, he thought, if she'd been off work for two days, she'd also been going that long without stealing breath from cups. "Want some?" he said, offering his.

She looked startled, pleased, and then, falsely unconcerned. She peered over the edge of his cup, shrugged, and said, "Okay, yeah, sure."

He handed it to her and politely watched the ducks so she could have some semblance of privacy with it. After a while she said thanks and handed it back to him. He nodded and stole a look at her profile again. It pleased him that her color already looked better. His breath had done that!

"Sorry about the other day," she said, "I was just . . ."

They waited together but she didn't finish the sentence.

"It's okay," he said, "I know I'm weird."

"No, you're, well—" she smiled, glanced at him, shrugged. "It isn't that. I like weird people. I'm weird. But, I mean, I'm not dead, okay? You kind of freaked me out with that."

He nodded. "Would you like to go out with me sometime?" Inwardly, he groaned. He couldn't believe he just said that.

"Listen, Alex?"

He nodded. Stop nodding, he told himself. Stop acting like a bobblehead.

"Why don't you tell me a little about yourself?"

So he told her. How he'd been coming to the park lately, watching people overfeed the ducks, wondering if he should tell them what they were doing but they all looked so happy doing it, and the ducks looked happy too, and he wasn't sure anyway, what if he was wrong, what if he told everyone to stop feeding bread to the ducks and it turned out it did them no harm and how would he know? Would they explode like balloons, or would it be more like how it had been when his wife died, a slow, painful death, eating her away inside, and how he used to come here, when he was a monk, well, not really a monk, he'd never gotten ordained or anything, but he'd been trying the idea on for a while and how he used to sing and spin in circles and how it felt a lot like what he'd remembered of happiness but he could never be sure because a remembered emotion is like a remembered taste, it's never really there. And then, one day, a real monk came and watched him spinning in circles and singing nonsense, and he just stood and watched Alex, which made him self-conscious because he didn't really know what he was doing, and the monk started laughing, which made Alex stop and the monk said, "Why'd you stop?" And Alex said, "I don't know what I'm doing." And the monk nodded, as if this was a very wise thing to say and this, just this monk with his round, bald head and wire-rimmed spectacles, in his simple orange robe (not at all like the orange-dyed sheet Alex was wearing) nodding when Alex said, "I don't know what I'm doing," made Alex cry and he and the monk sat down under that tree, and the monk (whose name was Ron) told him about Kali, the goddess who is both womb and grave. Alex felt like it was the first thing anyone had said to him that made sense since Tessie died and after that he stopped coming to the park, until just recently, and let his hair grow out again and stopped wearing his robe. Before she'd died, he'd been one of the lucky ones, or so he'd thought, because he made a small fortune in a dot com, and actually got out of it before it all went belly up while so many people he knew lost everything but then Tessie came home from her doctor's appointment, not pregnant, but with cancer, and he realized he wasn't lucky at all. They met in high school and were together until she died, at home, practically blind by that time and she made him promise he wouldn't just give up on life. So he began living this sort of half-life, but he wasn't unhappy or depressed, he didn't want her to think that, he just wasn't sure. "I sort of lost confidence in life," he said. "It's like I don't believe in it anymore. Not like suicide, but I mean, like the whole thing, all of it isn't real somehow. Sometimes I feel like it's all a dream, or a long nightmare that I can never wake up from. It's made me odd, I guess."

She bit her lower lip, glanced longingly at his cup.

"Here," Alex said, "I'm done anyway."

She took it and lifted it toward her face, breathing in, he was sure of it, and only after she was finished drinking the coffee. They sat like that in silence for a while and then they just started talking about everything, just as Alex had hoped they would. She told him how she had grown up living near the ocean, and her father had died young, and then her mother had too, and she had a boyfriend, her first love, who broke her heart, but the story she wrote was just a story, a story about her life, her dream life, the way she felt inside, like he did, as though somehow life was a dream. Even though everyone thought she was a painter (because he was the only one who read it, he was the only one who got it), she was a writer, not a painter, and stories seemed more real to her than life. At a certain point he offered to take the empty cup and throw it in the trash but she said she liked to peel off the wax, and then began doing so. Alex politely ignored the divergent ways she found to continue drinking his breath. He didn't want to embarrass her.

They finally stood up and stretched, walked through the park together and grew quiet, with the awkwardness of new friends. "You want a ride?" he said, pointing at his car.

She declined, which was a disappointment to Alex but he determined not to let it ruin his good mood. He was willing to leave it at that, to accept what had happened between them that afternoon as a moment of grace to be treasured and expect nothing more from it, when she said, "What are you doing next Tuesday?" They made a date, well, not a date, Alex reminded himself, an arrangement, to meet the following Tuesday in the park, which they did, and there followed many wonderful Tuesdays. They did not kiss. They were friends. Of course Alex still loved her. He loved her more. But he didn't bother her with all that and it was in the spirit of friendship that he suggested (after weeks of Tuesdays in the park) that the following Tuesday she come for dinner, "nothing fancy," he promised when he saw the slight hesitation on her face.

But when she said yes, he couldn't help it; he started making big plans for the night.

Naturally, things were awkward when she arrived. He offered to take her sweater, a lumpy looking thing in wild shades of orange, lime green, and purple. He should have just let her throw it across the couch, that would have been the casual non-datelike thing to do, but she handed it to him and then, wiping her hand through her hair, which, by candlelight looked like bloody grass, cased his place with those lavender eyes, deeply shadowed as though she hadn't slept for weeks.

He could see she was freaked out by the candles. He hadn't gone crazy or anything. They were just a couple of small candles, not even purchased from the store in the mall, but bought at the grocery store, unscented. "I like candles," he said, sounding defensive even to his own ears.

She smirked, as if she didn't believe him, and then spun away on the toes of her red sneaker and her green one, and plopped down on the couch. She looked absolutely exhausted. This was not a complete surprise to Alex. It had been a part of his plan, actually, but he felt bad for her just the same.

He kept dinner simple, lasagna, a green salad, chocolate cake for dessert. They didn't eat in the dining room. That would have been too formal. Instead they ate in the living room, she sitting on the couch, and he on the floor, their plates on the coffee table, watching a DVD of I Love Lucy episodes, a mutual like they had discovered. (Though her description of watching I Love Lucy reruns as a child did not gel with his picture of her in the crooked keeper's house, offering tea to melting ghosts, he didn't linger over the inconsistency.) Alex offered her plenty to drink but he wouldn't let her come into the kitchen, or get anywhere near his cup. He felt bad about this, horrible, in fact, but he tried to stay focused on the bigger picture.

After picking at her cake for a while, Agatha set the plate down, leaned back into the gray throw pillows, and closed her eyes.

Alex watched her. He didn't think about anything, he just watched her. Then he got up very quietly so as not to disturb her and went into the kitchen where he, carefully, quietly opened the drawer in which he had stored the supplies. Coming up from behind, eyeing her red and green hair, he moved quickly. She turned toward him, cursing loudly, her eyes wide and frightened, as he pressed her head to her knees, pulled her arms behind her back (to the accompaniment of a sickening crack, and her scream) pressed the wrists together and wrapped them with the rope. She struggled in spite of her weakened state, her legs flailing, kicking the coffee table. The plate with the chocolate cake flew off it and landed on the beige rug and her screams escalated into a horrible noise, unlike anything Alex had ever heard before. Luckily, Alex was prepared with the duct tape, which he slapped across her mouth. By that time he was rather exhausted himself. But she stood up and began to run, awkwardly, across the room. It broke his heart to see her this way. He grabbed her from behind. She kicked and squirmed but she was quite a small person and it was easy for him to get her legs tied.

"Is that too tight?" he asked.

She looked at him with wide eyes. As if he were the ghost.

"I don't want you to be uncomfortable."

She shook her head. Tried to speak, but only produced muffled sounds.

"I can take that off," he said, pointing at the duct tape. "But you have to promise me you won't scream. If you scream, I'll just put it on, and I won't take it off again. Though, you should know, ever since Tessie died I have these vivid dreams and nightmares, and I wake up screaming a lot. None of my neighbors has ever done anything about it. Nobody's called the police to report it, and nobody has even asked me if there's a problem. That's how it is amongst the living. Okay?"

She nodded.

He picked at the edge of the tape with his fingertips and when he got a good hold of it, he pulled fast. It made a loud ripping sound. She grunted and gasped, tears falling down her cheeks as she licked her lips.

"I'm really sorry about this," Alex said. "I just couldn't think of another way."

She began to curse, a string of expletives quickly swallowed by her weeping, until finally she managed to ask, "Alex, what are you doing?"

He sighed. "I know it's true, okay? I see the way you are, how tired you get and I know why. I know that you're a breath-stealer. I want you to understand that I know that about you, and I love you and you don't have to keep pretending with me, okay?"

She looked around the room, as if trying to find something to focus on. "Listen, Alex," she said, "Listen to me. I get tired all the time 'cause I'm sick. I didn't want to tell you, after what you told me about your wife. I thought it would be too upsetting for you. That's it. That's why I get tired all the time."

"No," he said, softly, "you're a ghost."

"I am not dead," she said, shaking her head so hard that her tears splashed his face. "I am not dead," she said over and over again, louder and louder until Alex felt forced to tape her mouth shut once more.

"I know you're afraid. Love can be frightening. Do you think I'm not scared? Of course I'm scared. Look what happened with Tessie. I know you're scared too. You're worried I'll turn out to be like Ezekiel, but I'm not like him, okay? I'm not going to hurt you. And I even finally figured out that you're scared 'cause of what happened with your mom. Of course you are. But you have to understand. That's a risk I'm willing to take. Maybe we'll have one night together or only one hour, or a minute. I don't know. I have good genes though. My parents, both of them, are still alive, okay? Even my grandmother only died a few years ago. There's a good chance I have a lot, and I mean a lot, of breath in me. But if I don't, don't you see, I'd rather spend a short time with you, than no time at all?"

He couldn't bear it, he couldn't bear the way she looked at him as if he were a monster when he carried her to the couch. "Are you cold?"

She just stared at him.

"Do you want to watch more *I Love Lucy*? Or a movie?"

She wouldn't respond. She could be so stubborn.

He decided on *Annie Hall*. "Do you like Woody Allen?" She just stared at him, her eyes filled with accusation. "It's a love story," he said, turning away from her to insert the DVD. He turned it on for her, then placed the remote control in her lap, which he realized was a stupid thing to do, since her hands were still tied behind her back, and he was fairly certain that, had her mouth not been taped shut, she'd be giving him that slack-jawed look of hers. She wasn't making any of this very easy. He picked the dish up off the floor, and the silverware, bringing them into the kitchen, where he washed them and the pots and pans, put aluminum foil on the leftover lasagna and put it into the refrigerator. After he finished sweeping the floor, he sat and watched the movie with her. He forgot about the sad ending. He always thought of it as a romantic comedy, never remembering the sad end. He turned off the TV and said, "I think it's late enough now. I think we'll be all right." She looked at him quizzically.

First Alex went out to his car and popped the trunk, then he went back inside where he found poor Agatha squirming across the floor. Trying to escape, apparently. He walked past her, got the throw blanket from the couch and laid it on the floor beside her, rolled her into it even as she squirmed and bucked. "Agatha, just try to relax," he said, but she didn't. Stubborn, stubborn, she could be so stubborn.

He threw her over his shoulder. He was not accustomed to carrying much weight and immediately felt the stress, all the way down his back to his knees. He shut the apartment door behind him and didn't worry about locking it. He lived in a safe neighborhood.

When they got to the car, he put her into the trunk, only then taking the blanket away from her beautiful face. "Don't worry, it won't be long," he said as he closed the hood.

He looked through his CDs, trying to choose something she would like, just in case the sound carried into the trunk, but he couldn't figure out what would be appropriate so he finally decided just to drive in silence.

It took about twenty minutes to get to the beach; it was late, and there was little traffic. Still, the ride gave him an opportunity to reflect on what he was doing. By the time he pulled up next to the pier, he had reassured himself that it was the right thing to do, even though it looked like the wrong thing.

He'd made a good choice, deciding on this place. He and Tessie used to park here, and he was amazed that it had apparently remained undiscovered by others seeking dark escape.

When he got out of the car he took a deep breath of the salt air and stood, for a moment, staring at the black waves, listening to their crash and murmur. Then he went around to the back and opened up the trunk. He looked over his shoulder, just to be sure. If someone were to discover him like this, his actions would be misinterpreted. The coast was clear, however. He wanted to carry Agatha in his arms, like a bride. Every time he had pictured it, he had seen it that way, but she was struggling again so he had to throw her over his shoulder where she continued to struggle. Well, she was stubborn, but he was too, that was part of the beauty of it, really. But it made it difficult to walk, and it was windier on the pier, also wet. All in all it was a precarious, unpleasant journey to the end.

He had prepared a little speech but she struggled against him so hard, like a hooked fish, that all he could manage to say was, "I love you," barely focusing on the wild expression in her face, the wild eyes, before he threw her in and she sank, and then bobbed up like a cork, only her head above the black waves, those eyes of hers, locked on his, and they remained that way, as he turned away from the edge of the pier and walked down the long plank, feeling lighter, but not in a good way. He felt those eyes, watching him, in the car as he flipped restlessly from station to station, those eyes, watching him, when he returned home, and saw the clutter of their night together, the burned-down candles, the covers to the *I Love Lucy* and *Annie Hall* DVDs on the floor, her crazy sweater on the dining room table, those eyes, watching him, and suddenly Alex was cold, so cold his teeth were chattering and he was shivering but sweating besides. The black water rolled over those eyes and closed them and he ran to the bathroom and only just made it in time, throwing up everything he'd eaten, collapsing to the floor, weeping, *What have I done? What was I thinking?*

He would have stayed there like that, he determined, until they came for him and carted him away, but after a while he became aware of the foul taste in his mouth. He stood up, rinsed it out, brushed his teeth and tongue, changed out of his clothes, and went to bed, where, after a good deal more crying, and trying to figure out exactly what had happened to his mind, he was amazed to find himself falling into a deep darkness like the water, from which, he expected, he would never rise.

But then he was lying there, with his eyes closed, somewhere between sleep and waking, and he realized he'd been like this for some time. Though he was fairly certain he had fallen asleep, something had woken him. In this half state, he'd been listening to the sound he finally recognized as dripping water. He hated it when he didn't turn the faucet tight. He tried to ignore it, but the dripping persisted. So confused was he that he even thought he felt a splash on his hand and another on his forehead. He opened one eye, then the other.

She stood there, dripping wet, her hair plastered darkly around her face, her eyes smudged black. "I found a sharp rock at the bottom of the world," she said and she raised her arms. He thought she was going to strike him, but instead she showed him the cut rope dangling there.

He nodded. He could not speak.

She cocked her head, smiled, and said, "Okay, you were right. You were right about everything. Got any room in there?"

He nodded. She peeled off the wet T-shirt and let it drop to the floor, revealing her small breasts white as the moon, unbuttoned and unzipped her jeans, wiggling seductively out of the tight, wet fabric, taking her panties off at the same time. He saw when she lifted her feet that the rope was no longer around them and she was already transparent below the knees. When she pulled back the covers he smelled the odd odor of saltwater and mud, as if she were both fresh and loamy. He scooted over, but only far enough that when she eased in beside him, he could hold her, wrap her wet cold skin in his arms, knowing that he was offering her everything, everything he had to give, and that she had come to take it.

"You took a big risk back there," she said.

He nodded.

She pressed her lips against his and he felt himself growing lighter, as if all his life he'd been weighed down by this extra breath, and her lips were cold but they grew warmer and warmer and the heat between them created a steam until she burned him and still, they kissed, all the while Alex thinking, I love you, I love you, I love you, until, finally, he could think it no more, his head was as light as his body, lying beside her, hot flesh to hot flesh, the cinder of his mind could no longer make sense of it, and he hoped, as he fell into a black place like no other he'd ever been in before, that this was really happening, that she was really here, and the suffering he'd felt for so long was finally over.

The Machine

(May Day)

WHEN ALL THE WORLD IS DARK AND THE BLOS-somed flowers have folded petals to closed bud and the butterflies sleep, and the deer, and the sheep; while bats unfurl and eat the night and frighten humans who do not like what they devour or, what they are; the nightingale sings. Lovers pause in tumbled sheets and hold that song in their gaze. God smiles on us, they say and return to embrace of limb and soul, or at least limb, and, of course, forget everything in that waking sleep of sex or love, the waking sleep of humans; not just lovers but children in their candy games and Pokeman hours, teenagers glued to the power of screens, TV, computer, the messy world of tactile sensation diverged; and even the old, who forget what the toaster is for, but maintain a sort of creaky wisdom, if anyone would listen between the obvious confusion of words, even they, if their hearing aids are turned just right, hear the nightingale song and think, How nice, what beauty. Who remembers why? Perhaps it's best it remains unspoken. Why uproot the beautiful flower to expose its ugly source? Why remember the song's inception? Why remember anything but love, and joy, and, of course, e-mail addresses and where the remote control is?

High schools still insist on a history prerequisite for graduation but let's face it, our brightest minds are not in Universities bent over papyrus and yellow-paged books, but surfing the Web and unleashing the awesome power of space, selling the present for brighter teeth and mobile lives and what's really important here? Ghosts? Even those that drop feathers (germy, potentially full of disease) and sing golden songs in the dark? Very nice. But what's the point?

Graveyards creak with too many bones, and the weight of headstones, and when the wind blows the air is dusty with the dead. Ah life, its hoary inevitability. What's the point? Progress promises, as it always has, immortality, but for now there is only life and it points to death and after that, there are all sorts of theories, but the only thing certain is decay, the rattle of bones and dust. So who can blame us for loving the nightingale's song in the dark and forgetting the rest?

THE STORY OF THE NIGHTINGALE'S SONG

Philomela and Procne are sisters who play in the grass or by the stream from a time when children played like that, with each other and imagination. But let's not get too sentimental here. Things happened then that today, in all our imperfect knowledge, we would never thrust upon a young girl. Right? For instance, once, when there was a plague of locusts, green-eyed and scrying, the earth undulating with their greedy mandibles, a friend of theirs who menstruated in the corner of her house was forced out to walk amongst the insects and bleed over the crunch of them beneath her bare feet, to cast away the plague, with her womanly power, which was not immediately successful, and when she returned, weeping and bitten, locusts in her hair and on her skirt, the adults swatted at her as if she was one of them, until all the locusts were corpses, and in a way she was too, her eyes like shallow water.

And there was war. Great and savage battles where men actually saw who they killed and even had the blood of the dead on their hands and it splattered on their faces, in their beards, and it took weeks sometimes to comb it all out. The girls' father, Pandion, was in just such a war, even as they played by the stream, he fought for the reason humans still fight.

In frustration Pandion calls for a mercenary, a great fighter who will help him to win and Tereus takes the job and slays some men and also plots battle strategies that win the war. Tereus combs the blood from his beard with bones of Pandion's slain, and when the other men complain, he laughs, because to him, it's all the same. The dead are the dead, and that is the only victory.

Pandion thinks Tereus is like a son. A great warrior son. Come home with me, he says, we will settle payment there. You will feast with us and celebrate. Tereus doesn't really care but he is hungry and likes the sound of sleeping in a bed, though in reality this disappoints him and soon he has set up a tent on the castle grounds which everyone thinks is really funny but nobody comments on, except the girls, who are innocent, and do not understand what Tereus does for a living.

What Tereus does now is sit in the tent and sharpen his swords and watch the girls playing by the stream. Procne, the older, her hair in a braid that comes undone as she runs in her muslin, still shaped more like bones than woman, and the little one, Philomela, her red hair long and in wild disarray of grass and clover, her dress stained with green, her little girl laughter and screams larking through the meadow, and for a moment Tereus stops sharpening and something like a smile plays at his lips.

Pandion, seeing this, celebrates the obvious. It is clear what Tereus wants for payment. Tereus nods, it's true, and there's no shame in it, for there's no shame in him. When Pandion brings the wrong daughter, the older one, Procne, he accepts her. What does it really matter? One thing Tereus knows is a body is just a body, one much the same as the other. Blood and bone. Skin and hair. Teeth.

What a wedding! What a feast! Roasted hummingbirds, and roasted larks. Sugared flowers and stag's blood, and twelve pipers, and mead, pomegranates, and shank of deer and lamb and cakes decorated with violets; and dancing girls, and the young bride, her cheeks red as apples, her rounded lips, her eyes all shining. All this for me? she thinks. Then glances at Tereus. He sits grinning, the great warrior, watching Philomela, a brother to her now. What did they mean, the ladies who dressed her, warning her of his sword's sharp thrust? He grins and claps. My husband, she thinks, I shall not fear him, he is dangerous only in war.

Well, innocence. Even now, we have our innocence. In spite of the worst that we know of ourselves, we still have innocence. The nightingale's song, for instance. We hear only that, and forget the rest, just as generations to come will remember Columbine only as a flower.

So Procne had her innocence and it was thrust from her, given up by her father to Tereus who enjoyed it, I guess you could say. Joy may not be the right word. At any rate, they were married and the marriage was consummated. He took her to Dailus, which lay in the high pass and she soon gave birth, in a torment of blood and pain, to Itys. She suckled baby and husband until her breasts were always sore and between these tasks she did needlework and thought often of her sister, dear, dear Philomela, who plays beside the stream and pretended they were still together, while Tereus, in a battle-free period, wandered restless through the fields, slicing wildflowers with his sword and also thinking of Philomela, her glorious red hair, her little girl smile.

When Tereus leaves, unexplained, to bring Philomela to Dailus, Procne does not guess the reason for his absence but shifts Itys to the right breast and remarks to the suckling babe, that whatever the reason for his departure, she is glad of it. Oh, but if only she could see her dear sister once more.

Why is it that evil is good's opportunity? If only Tereus was speaking the truth when he told Pandion that Procne missed her sister so much he had come for her, to bring her to her sister as a sort of May Day gift. If only, as Philomela squealed with delight and packed her little sack with muslin dresses and needlework and flower garlands and colored ribbons, Tereus, who waited in the hall with Pandion, was thinking of bringing Philomela to her sister, of Procne's smile, instead of Philomela's pretty lips. If only he was interested in happiness.

Philomela is going on a journey! Philomela is going to see her sister. Goodbye Nurse, Goodbye Cook, Goodbye little dog. Goodbye birds, goodbye Papa, goodbye, goodbye house, goodbye stream, goodbye meadow.

Goodbye everything she ever was and dreamt of, though she does not know this as Tereus helps her to his horse, and wraps his great arms around her. Goodbye innocence. Goodbye.

Somewhere between Pandion's castle and Dailus it happens. He takes her into the forest where she chats happily as she picks flowers for her sister until Tereus pushes her to the ground and rapes her. How much shall be described? The sky was blue with two fat clouds, one in the shape of a bird, the other like a sleeping dog. The ground was bumpy and a sharp stick jutted in her back. The sun shone through the leaves, which dappled color, as if she was a fish in the stream. There was one flower just near enough to observe closely, purple lips and a red center; the green stem bent slightly, a tiny white bug on the second leaf. When Tereus is finished he is not completely satisfied. This girl talks too much. He cuts out her tongue and casts it into the brush. She screams and bleeds and weeps. He salves the wound with curing plants he stuffs in her mouth and then, he rapes her again. The birds sing, the horse paws at the ground, a chipmunk twitters in a tree, a squirrel scurries past but she is silent. When he removes the curing leaves the bleeding has stopped. He mounts the horse, pulls her up in front of him. They continue on their journey to Dailus.

Why remember? Why tell this tale of horror? Why does evil happen? Why does it happen so often to children and what does the nightingale have to do with this tongueless child, this evil act, this sister with Itys at her breast who, like his father, never seems satisfied.

Tereus brings Philomela to Dailus but he does not bring her home. Rather, he brings her to his house in the country, where he locks her in a room. He hires good servants who are comfortable with keys, and unquestioning of tongueless, imprisoned girls, to bring her food and water, silks and threads to keep herself busy in between him until at last he leaves. She watches him from the window, riding away on his horse, she watches his great arms and broad back recede to a dot until he is gone and then she begins stitching, a picture story of sorts. When words are taken, what remains?

She sends back the trays of bread and cheese, meat and fruit. The cook frowns at the empty water bowl. What will happen if the prisoner dies while the master is gone? It is clear that is not his intention. Next meal the cook outdoes herself and prepares a meal of roasted quail stuffed with chestnuts and sliced apples dipped in honey and a bowl of sunflower seeds and millet. This time when the tray is returned the roasted quail is untouched and the sliced apples are brown and there are two flics in the honey but the sunflower-millet bowl is empty except for a small stitched cloth of a red-haired girl smiling and this is the first time anyone, ever, has given the cook a present. The next day Philomela's tray has four bowls of sunflower seeds and millet and even a little flower which is meant as decoration, but comes back with a crushed appearance as though Philomela had thrust it to her lips for its nectar so the next day the cook sends several flowers and six bowls of sunflower seeds and millet and all the flowers come back crushed, and five of the bowls empty and in the corner of the tray is a small square of fabric stitched with the picture of a sun, even though the day is rainy. The cook puts the fabric into her apron pocket and imagines collecting dozens of them and stitching them into a quilt.

And perhaps that's what would have happened, if that's all there was to Philomela's needlework, but in her lonely little room she stitched the sad story of the girls playing, a wedding, the red-haired girl alone, the groom's return, the girl with him on the horse, the flowers she was picking, the man astride the girl, the knife near her throat, the tongue held up, the girl weeping, the house in the country, the window with the girl sitting in it, sewing. This she wrapped in a muslin dress and tied with ribbon addressed to her sister, returned on the tray with another package for the cook, who paid a messenger boy from her own savings to deliver the package safely and then unwrapped hers, a lovely shawl stitched with daisies which she took to wrapping around her shoulders at night, in her lonely little room off the kitchen, and even if no one saw, and it didn't make sense to wear it, she loved to do this, and it became her favorite time of day, though never, for even one moment, did it occur to her to free the girl.

When Procne receives the package, she recognizes the muslin dress it is wrapped in and unfurls the ribbon eagerly. Itys sleeps, a rare occasion, and Tereus has gone to work, so for Procne this is a moment of peace, and now this missive from her sister, a moment of joy. She unfurls the ribbon, shakes out the cloth and reads the pictures in horror. She understands every unspoken word, every stitch. She recognizes the little house in the country, not even a day's distance. She brings Itys to the wet nurse who secretly moans when she sees the greedy suckler and his mother approaching, mounts her horse and rides to free her sister, her little tongueless sister, who used to sing and chat so happily. Procne rides and plots endlessly. Revenge.

The human need for balance. Restitution. The endless accounting of gain and loss. The urge to unburden the evil act, return it to its source. What to do for the tongueless girl?

When Philomela hears the horse approaching she weeps in the corner of her room, she curls up into herself, like a little bird, her head beneath her arms, her bony elbows jutted out, she tries to make herself smaller and smaller as the footsteps approach and the keys rattle. When the door opens she does not look until she hears, no, it cannot be, but yes, she hears her sister's voice. "Philomela," her name lovingly spoken. She raises her face of tears and sees Procne, her dark hair wild from the ride; her purple gown all wrinkled, just as she used to be in the meadow, by the stream. Behind her stands the cook, her white pasty mouth open, the ring of keys in her doughy hands.

Procne bends to embrace her and Philomela flinches but then

remembers who is with her and leans into the loving arms. Procne holds her and thinks how weightless she has become, as if her tongue was what held her to the earth. She carries her out of the room and down the stairs and out the door to a horse, saddled and waiting as ordered. This she mounts with Philomela before her, a tiny package, a little girl, a living wound. She gallops off leaving only dust and the cook who dabs her eyes and wipes her nose and goes back inside to her pot of onion soup.

Procne brings Philomela to her house. Not their father's, but who can blame her for this choice? After all, it is their father who gave them to Tereus, he should not have been so gullible. At any rate, it is clear this matter rests in their hands. Tereus is still away, killing the enemy, no that's not right, Procne amends, Tereus is still away killing. It is hard to remember that he has no enemy, only those he is paid to kill and those he is not, and they are interchangable. What ever was her father thinking to give her to such a man?

Procne retrieves Itys from the wet nurse and he immediately cries and grabs at her breast. She unlaces and lets him suckle greedily. Philomela flits about the room and shakes her head at the various plans of revenge Procne offers until at last, in exasperation, Procne says, "Well, what?" Philomela raises one small, white hand and points at Itys who suckles with wide-open eyes, the color of his father's. Procne looks down at him and finds the answer to the question she most often thinks when he is suckling, will this never end? Will he want me with his teeth? She looks up at Philomela, who stands beside the fire, and she nods. Yes. Itys.

When news arrives of Tereus's return from battle, Philomela hides in a great basket in the corner, curled up as if in a nest, and Procne turns the roasted meat on the spit, well done, they thought he'd return sooner, but, this isn't really about appetite anyway.

He roars into the house, the great beast of a man. Dried blood clings to his beard and eyebrows. He is hungry and lusty and says he will eat, then have her and then, he thinks he needs some time in the country. She feeds him the roasted child. He devours it . . . innocently. When done, he pats his full stomach, undoes his belt and this is when Philomela rises from the basket and he realizes he's been found out. But oh well, he's still the master. Then, Procne tells him.

"You just ate Itys."

He roars, as you can imagine. He reaches for the fire ax and chases them, two sisters, whose victory seems rather short. They are weeping, and he is screaming and the gods see this and decide it must be put to a stop. Why now, and not sooner? Where were they when he raped Philomela in the woods? Where were they when he cut out her tongue? Where were they when Itys reached for his mother's breast and she unsheathed the knife instead? Where are the gods most of the time? Oh well, the ways of the gods we humans cannot understand. But at last they stop it, with a wave of godly hands. Tereus is changed to a hawk, Procne a swallow, and Philomela, well, you've guessed it, a nightingale.

Later, the child's bones are found by the cook who unwittingly feeds them to the dogs. She thinks they have all gone to the house in the country and the cook there, wrapped in her daisy shawl, and fingering the fabric stitched of a smiling girl, thinks they all remain in town, and the hawk swoops down to catch a gopher, the swallow flies to Capistrano, and the nightingale discovers, on one dark and starry night, that she can sing, so she does.

At close, the questions remain. Why do people hurt each other? Is evil someone born, or something between us, something ephemeral that grows in circumstance that allows it? Why do girls and women, even today, in our modern and knowledgeable world suffer rape, and mutilation? Why does any one suffer? And what does fable, myth, story have to do with these important questions, certainly worthy of a search on the Web in between those auction sites where there are some really good deals, and at least the questions are real and the merchandise is real, even movies are real, sort of, because they have real people in them at least, but fiction? What's the point? Everyone knows a bird is just a bird, a song is just a song, a story, just a story. Why pretend it means anything?

How do stories help us solve the terrible riddle of being human? How do we take all our suffering, the rapes, and wars, and children dying, and turn it into something like a bird song in the night? How do we become better than we've been? And how do we get from here to there, when the gods seem so reluctant to help? Could it be, even they don't know the answers?

Maybe inquiry isn't what we need. Maybe the more we pick at the fabric of our beliefs, we find how fragile it all really is, and how there's nothing behind the cloth except empty space, an infinite sky that cannot support the gravity of our assertions, how weightless we become without them. Maybe it's better not to think about that.

Maybe it is just enough to know that the nightingale was once a brutalized child, and when all the world is dark, she sings.

Evidence of Love in a Case of Abandonment: One Daughter's Personal Account

(Mother's Day)

"*W*HEN I, OR PEOPLE LIKE ME, ARE RUNNING THE country, you'd better flee, because we will find you, we will try you, and we'll execute you. I mean every word of it. I will make it part of my mission to see to it that they are tried and executed."

Randall Terry, founder of Operation Rescue

It took a long time to deduce that many of the missing women could not be accounted for. Executions were a matter of public record then and it was still fairly easy to keep track of them. They were on every night at seven o'clock, filmed from the various execution centers. It was policy back then to name the criminal as the camera lingered over her face. Yet women went missing who never appeared on execution. Rumors started. Right around then some of the policies changed. The criminals were no longer named, and execution centers sprung up all over the country so it was no longer possible to account for the missing. The rumors persisted though, and generally took one of two courses; Agents were using the criminals for their own nefarious purposes, or women were sneaking away and assembling an army.

When my mother didn't come home, my father kept saying she must have had a meeting he'd forgotten about, after all, she volunteered for Homeland Security's Mothers in Schools program, as well as did work for the church, and the library. That's my mom. She always has to keep busy. When my father started calling hospitals, his freckles all popped out against his white skin the way they get when he's upset, and I realized he was hoping she'd had an accident, I knew. The next morning, when I found him sitting in the rocker, staring out the picture window, their wedding album in his lap, I really knew.

Of course I am not the only abandoned daughter. Even here, there are a few of us. We are not marked in any way a stranger could see, but we are known in our community. Things are better for those whose mothers are executed. They are a separate group from those of us whose mothers are unaccounted for, who may be so evil as to escape reparation for their crimes, so sick as to plan to attack the innocent ones left behind.

I am obsessed with executions, though there are too many to keep track of, hard as I try to flip through the screens and have them all going on at once. I search for her face. There are many faces. Some weeping, some screaming, some with lips trembling, or nostrils flaring, but I never see her face. Jenna Offeren says her mother was executed in Albany but she's lying. Jenna Offeren is a weak, annoying person but I can't completely blame her. Even my own father tried it. One morning he comes into my room, sits at the edge of my bed and says, "Lisle, I'm sorry. I saw her last night. Your mother. They got her." I just shook my head. "Don't try to make me feel better," I said, "I know she's still alive."

My mother and I, we have that thing some twins have. That's how close we've always been. Once, when I was still a little kid, I fell from a tree at Sarah T.'s house and my mom came running into the backyard, her hair a mess, her lipstick smeared, before Mrs. T. had even finished dialing the cell. "I just knew," mom said, "I was washing the windows and all of a sudden I had this pain in my stomach and I knew you needed me. I came right over." My wrist was broke (and to this day hurts when it's going to rain) and I couldn't do my sewing or synchronized swimming for weeks, but I almost didn't mind because, back then I thought me and mom had something special between us, and what happened with my wrist proved it. Now I'm not so sure. Everything changes when your mother goes missing.

I look for her face all the time. Not just on the screens but on the heads of other women, not here, of course, but if we go to

Milwaukee, or on the school trip to Chicago, I look at every women's face, searching for hers. I'm not the only one either. I caught Jenna Offeren doing the same thing, though she denied it. (Not mine, of course. Hers.)

Before she left us, Mom was not exactly a happy person, but what normal American girl goes around assuming that her own mother is a murderer? She even helped me with my project in seventh year, cutting out advertisements that used that model, Heidi Eagle, who was executed the year before, and I remember, so clearly, mom saying that Heidi's children would have been beautiful, so how was I to know that my own mother was one of the evil doers?

But then what did I think was going on with all that crying? My mother cried all the time. She cried when she was doing the dishes, she cried when she cleaned the toilets, she even cried in the middle of laughing, like the time I told her about Mr. Saunders demonstrating to us girls what it's like to be pregnant with a basketball. The only time I can ever remember my mom saying anything traceable, anything that could be linked from our perfect life to the one I'm stuck in now, was when she found a list of boys names on my T.S.O. and asked if they were boys I had crushes on. I don't know what she was thinking to say such a thing because there were seven names on that list and I am not a slut, but anyhow, I explained that they were baby names I was considering for when my time came and she got this look on her face like maybe she'd been a hologram all along and was just going to fade away and then she said, "When I was your age, I planned on being an astronaut."

My cheeks turned bright red, of course. I was embarrassed for her to talk like that. She tried to make light of it by looking over the list, letting me know which names she liked (Liam and Jack) and which she didn't (Paul and Luke). If the time ever comes (and I am beginning to have my doubts that it will) I'm going to choose one of the names she hated. It's not much, but it's all I have. There's only so much you can do to a mother who is missing.

My father says I'm spending too much time watching screens so he has insisted that we do something fun together, "as a family" he said, trying to make it sound cheerful like we aren't the lamest excuse for family you've ever seen, just me and him.

There's plenty of families without mothers, of course. Apparently this was initially a surprise to Homeland Security, it was generally assumed that those women who had abortions during the dark times never had any children, but a lot of women of my mother's generation were swayed by the evil propaganda of their youth, had abortions and careers even, before coming back to the light of righteous behavior. So having an executed mother is not necessarily that bad. There's a whole extra shame in being associated with a mother who is missing however, out there somewhere, in a militia or something. (With the vague possibility that she is not stockpiling weapons and learning about car bombs, but captured by one of the less ethical Agents, but what's the real chance of that? Isn't that just a fantasy kids like Jenna Offeren came up with because they can't cope?) At any rate, to counteract the less palatable rumor, and the one that puts the Agents in the worse light, Homeland Security has recently begun the locks of hair program. Now they send strands of criminal's hair to the family and it's become a real trend for the children to wear it in see-through lockets. None of this makes sense, of course. The whole reason the executions became anonymous in the first place was to put to rest the anarchist notion that some women had escaped their fate, but Homeland Security is not the department of consistency (I think I can say that) and seems to lean more toward a policy of confusion. The locks of hair project has been very successful and has even made some money as families are now paying to have executed women's corpses dug up for their hair. At any rate, you guessed it, Jenna shows up at execution with a lock of hair necklace that she says comes from her mother but I know it's Jenna's own hair, which is blonde and curly while her mom's was brownish gray. "That's 'cause she dyed it," Jenna says. I give up. Nobody dyes their hair brownish gray. Jenna has just gone completely nuts.

It seems like the whole town is at execution and I realize my father's right, I've been missing a lot by watching them on screen all the time. "Besides, it's starting to not look right, never going. It was different when your mother was still with us," he said. So I agreed, though I didn't expect much. I mean no way would they execute my mom right here in her hometown. Sure, it happens but it would be highly unlikely, so what's the point? I expected it to be incredibly boring like church, or the meetings of The Young Americans, or Home Ec class but it wasn't anything like any of that. Screens really give you no idea of the excitement of an execution and if you, like me, think that you've seen it all because you've been watching it on screen for years, I recommend you attend your own hometown event. It just might surprise you. Besides, it's important to stay active in your community.

We don't have a stadium, of course, not in a town of a population of eight thousand and dwindling, so executions are held on the football field the first Wednesday of every month. I was surprised by the screens displayed around the field but my father said that was the only way you could get a real good look at the faces, and he was right. It was fascinating to look at the figure in the center of the field, how small she looked, to the face on the screen, freakishly large. Just like on screen at home, the women were all ages from grandmothers to women my mother's age and a few probably younger. The problem is under control now. No one would think of getting an abortion. There's already talk about cutting back the program in a few years and I feel kind of sentimental about it. I've grown up with executions and can't imagine what kids will watch instead. Not that I would wish this on anyone. It's a miserable thing to be in my situation. Maybe no one will even want me now. I ask my dad about this on the way to execution, what happens to girls like me and for a while he pretends he doesn't know what I'm talking about until I spell it out and he can't act all Homeland Security. He shakes his head and sighs. "It's too soon to say, Lisle. Daughters of executed moms, they've done all right, maybe you know, not judges wives, or Agents, or anyone like that, but they've had a decent time of it for the most part. Daughters of missing moms, well, it's just too soon to tell. Hey, maybe you'll get to be a breeder." He says it like it's a good thing, giving up my babies every nine or ten months.

"I hate mom," I say. He doesn't scold me. After all, what she did, she did to both of us.

It seems like the whole town is here, though I know this can't be right because it's the first time I've come since I was a kid, and that would be statistically improbable if we were the only ones who never came back, but, even though I am certain it's not the whole town, I'd have to say it's pretty close to it. Funny how in all these faces and noise and excitement I can see who's wearing locks of hair lockets as if they are made of shining light, which of course they are not. I could forgive her, I think—and I'm surprised by the tears in my eyes—if she'd just do the right thing and turn herself in. Maybe I'm not being fair. After all, maybe she's trapped somewhere, held prisoner by some Agent and there's nothing she can do about it. I, too, take comfort in this little fantasy from time to time.

Each execution is done individually. She walks across the entire field in a hood. The walk takes a long time 'cause of the shackles.

I can think of no reasonable explanation for the hood, beyond suspense. It is very effective. The beginning of the walk is a good time to take a bathroom break or get a snack, that's how long it takes. No one wants to be away from his seat when the criminal gets close to the red circle at the center of the field. The closer she gets to the circle (led by one of the Junior Agents, or, as is the case tonight, by one of the children from the town's various civic programs) the more quiet it gets until eventually the only noise is the sound of chains. I've heard this on screen a million times but then there is neighborhood noise going on, cars, maybe someone talking on a cell, dogs barking, that sort of thing, but when the event is live there's no sound other than maybe a cough or a baby crying. I have to tell you all those people in the same space being quiet, the only sound the chains rattling around the criminal's ankles and wrists, well it's way more powerful than how it seems on screen. She always stands for a few seconds in the center of the circle but she rarely stands still. Once placed in position, hands and feet shackled, she displays her fear by wavering, or the shoulders go up, sometimes she is shaking so bad you can see it even if you're not looking on screen.

The child escort walks away to polite applause and the Executioner comes to position. He unties the hood, pauses for dramatic effect (and it is dramatic!) then plucks the hood off, which almost always causes some of her hair to stand out from her head, as though she's been electrocuted, or taken off a knit cap on a snowy day, and at that moment we turn to the screen to get a closer look. I never get bored of it. The horror on their faces, the dripping nostrils, the spit bubbling from lips, the eyes wet with tears, wide with terror. Occasionally there is a stoic one, but there aren't many of these, and when there is, it's easy enough to look away from the screen and focus on the big picture. What had she been thinking? How could she murder someone so tiny, so innocent, and not know she'd have to pay? When I think of what the time from before was like I shudder and thank God for being born in the Holy times. In spite of my mother, I am blessed. I know this, even though I sometimes forget. Right there, in the football field bleachers I fold my hands and bow my head. When I am finished my father is giving me a strange look. "If this is too upsetting we can leave," he says. He constantly makes mistakes like this. Sometimes I just ignore him, but this time I try to explain. "I just realized how lucky I am." I can't think of what else to say, how to make him understand so I simply smile. Right then the stoic woman is shot. When I look I see the gaping maul that was her head, right where that evil thought was first conceived to destroy the innocent life that grew inside her. Now she is neither stoic nor alive. She lies in a heap, twitching for a while, but those are just nerves.

It's getting late. Some people use this time to usher their young children home. When we came, all those years ago, my mom letting me play with her gold chain while I sat in her lap, we were one of the first to leave, though I was not the youngest child in attendance. My mother was always strict that way. "Time for bed," she said cheerfully, first to me, and then by way of explanation, pressing my head tight against her shoulder, trying to make me look tired, pressing so hard that I started crying, which, I now realize, served her purpose.

My father says he has to use the bathroom. There is a pocket of space around me when he leaves. My father is gone a long time. This is unusual for the men's bathroom and I must admit I get a little worried about him, especially as the woman approaches the target circle but right when I am starting to think he's going to be too late, he comes, his head bent low so as not to obstruct the view. He sits beside me at what is the last possible second. He shrugs and looks like he's about to say something. Horrified, I turn away. It would be just like him to talk at a time like this.

The girl (from the Young and Beautiful club) dressed all in white with a flower wreathe on her head (and a locks of hair locket glimmering on her chest) walks away from the woman. The tenor of applause grows louder as the Executioner approaches. We are trying to show how much we've appreciated his work tonight. The Executioners are never named. They travel in some kind of secret rotation so no one can ever figure it out, but over time they get reputations. They wear masks, of course, or they would always be hounded for autographs, but are recognized, when they are working, by the insignia on their uniforms. This one is known as Red Dragon for the elaborate dragon on his chest. The applause can be registered on the criminal who shakes like jello. She shakes so much that it is not unreasonable to wonder if she will be one of the fainters. I hate the fainters. They mess with the dramatic arc, all that buildup of the long walk, the rattling chains, the Executioner's arrival, only to have the woman fall in a large heap on the ground. Sometimes it takes forever to revive her, and some effort to get her to stand, at which point the execution is anti-climatic.

The Executioner, perhaps sensing this very scenario, says something to jello woman that none of us can hear but she suddenly goes still. There is scattered applause for Red Dragon's skill. He turns toward the audience, and, though he wears his mask, there is something in his demeanor that hushes the crowd. We are watching a master at work. Next, he steps in front of the woman, reaches with both hands around her neck, creating the effect of a man about to give a kiss. We are all as still as if we are waiting for that kiss. With one gesture, he unties the string, and in the same breath reaches up and pulls off the hood. We gasp.

Mrs. Offeren's face fills the screen. Someone screams. I think it is Jenna. I am torn between looking for her in the crowd, and keeping my attention on her mother, whose head turns at the sound so there is only a view of her giant ear but the Executioner says something sharp and she snaps her head back to attention. The screen betrays that her eyes peer past the Executioner, first narrow then wide, and her lips part at the moment she realizes she is home. Her eyes just keep moving after that, searching the crowd, looking for Jenna, I figure, until suddenly, how can it be suddenly when it happens like this every time, but it is suddenly, her head jerks back with the firecracker sound of the shot, she falls from the screen. She lies on the ground, twitching, the red puddle blossoming around her head. Jenna screams and screams. It is my impression that no one does anything to stop her. Nor does anyone use this break to go to the snack shop, or the bathroom, or home. I don't know when my father's hand has reached across the space between us but at some point I realize it rests, gently, on my thigh, when I look at him, he squeezes, lightly, almost like a woman would, as though there is no strength left inside him. They quickly cut some of Mrs. Offeren's hair before it gets too bloody, and bag it, lift her up, clumsily so that at first her arm and then her head falls toward the ground (the assistants are tired by this time of night) load her into the cart. We listen to the sound of the wheels that need to be oiled and the faint rattle of chains as the cart lumbers across the field. Jenna weeps audibly. The center of the red circle is coated in blood. I pretend it is a Roarshack and decide it looks exactly like a pterodactyl. The cleaning crew comes and hoses it down. That's when people start moving about, talk, rush to the bathroom, take sleeping children home, but it goes mostly silent again when the Offeren family stands up. The seven of them sidle down the bleacher and walk along the side of the field.

I watch the back of Jenna's head, her blonde curls under the lights, almost golden like a halo, though no one, not even the most forgiving person is ever going to mistake Jenna for someone holy. Her mother was a murderer, after all. Yet I realize she'll soon replace that stupid fake locket with a real one while I have nothing. She might even get to marry a Police or a trash collector, even a teacher, while the best I can hope for is a position at one of the orphanages. My dad's idea that I might be a breeder someday seems highly optimistic.

"Let's go," I say.

"Are you sure? Maybe the next one . . ." but he doesn't even finish the thought. He must see something in my face that tells him I am done with childish fantasies.

She's never coming back. Whatever selfish streak caused her, all those years ago to kill one child is the same selfish streak that allows her to abandon me now.

We walk down the bleachers. Everyone turns away from us, holding their little kids close. My father walks in front of me, with his head down, his hands in his pocket. By the time we get to the car in the parking lot we can hear the polite applause from the football field as another woman enters the circle. He opens his door. I open mine. We drive home in silence. I crane my neck to try to look up at the sky as if I expect to find something there, God maybe, or the living incarnation of the blood pterodactyl but of course I see neither. There is nothing. I close my eyes and think of my mother. Oh, how I miss her.

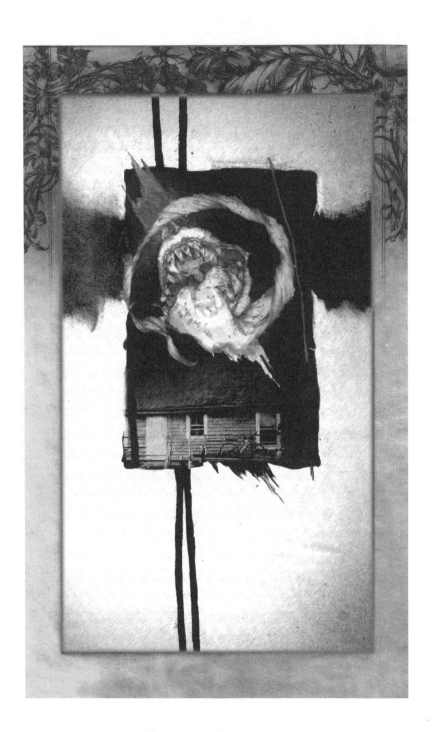

Don't Ask

(Father's Day)

*W*HEN THE LOST BOYS RETURNED WITH THEIR piercings, tattoos, and swagger, we rejoiced and greeted them with balloons, bubble gum, chocolate chip cookies, and bone crunching hugs, which they did not resist. Only later did we realize that this was one of their symptoms, this acquiescence, not a sign of their affection for us, though we do not doubt their affection.

How could wolves slope through town, unseen, and steal our boys from bicycles, from country roads, from the edge of the driveway, from our kitchen tables, dank with the scent of warm milk and soggy cereal; from our arms—wasn't it just yesterday that we held our boys close and sang them lullabies? How could they be taken from us?

Yet they were, and we wept and gnashed our teeth, tore our hair and screamed their names into the dark. Through the seasons we searched for them so thoroughly that even in our dreams we could not rest and often awoke to find dewy grass stuck to the soles of our feet, dirt beneath our fingernails, our hair matted by the wind. We continued to search even after the sheriff, with his hound dog face and quivering hands, said he would never stop looking but couldn't keep meeting with us and the very next day we woke up and no one waited at the door with pots of coffee and boxes of sticky, bright-colored doughnuts, and we sat at our kitchen tables and listened to school busses pass, not even slowing down for the memory of our sons.

But why speak about sorrow now that our boys have returned? They are home again, sleeping with hairy feet hanging over the edges of little boy beds, wearing the too small T-shirts, the split pants that reveal their long bones and taut muscles which quiver and spasm while they dream.

Of course we realized that in the years our boys were gone they had grown, this was the hope at least, this was the best possibility of all the horrible scenarios, that our lost boys were growing in the wolves den and not slaughtered by them—so yes, we are happy, of course we are, but what is this strange sorrow we discover in the dark? Why can't we stop weeping during this, the happiest of times?

Years before our boys returned there was the return of the famous lost boy, stolen from the end of his driveway, the wheels of his blue bicycle still spinning when his mother went to the door to call him in for dinner and saw the bike there but did not immediately comprehend it as a sign of catastrophe. He was missing for eight years, and was a hero for a while, until he started committing petty crimes in the neighborhood.

The famous lost boy, a man now, explains that he has been observing our behavior and the behavior of our sons. We cannot help but feel squeamish about the whole thing, we are uncomfortable with the notion that, after everything that happened, we have been studied and observed and did not know it. We discuss this in whispers in the high school auditorium, where the famous lost boy has come to speak. The therapists have their theories but we assume only one person has the truth and we are eager to hear what he can tell us about all our suffering, because, we say, nodding our heads and hugging ourselves in the cold auditorium, this happened to all of us.

"No," the famous lost boy (now a grown man with long, stringy hair) says. "It didn't."

We have been advised by therapists and counselors, experts beyond the meager fourth grade education of the famous lost boy (by the time he came back, he was too angry and unruly for school) not to ask what happened. "They will tell you when they are ready," the experts say.

We ask them if they want maple syrup for their pancakes, what show they'd like to watch, what games they'd like to play. We spoil them and expect them to revel in it, the way they did before they were taken, but oddly, in spite of all they've been through, and the horrors they have endured, they behave as though our servitude and their eminence is a given. Yet, sometimes we ask a question, so innocent, "Chocolate chip or peanut butter?" which they respond to with confusion, frowning as if trying to guess a right answer, or as though unfamiliar with the terms. Other times they bark or growl like an angry dog being taunted, but it passes so quickly we are sure it's been imagined.

The famous lost boy wants us to give him our sons. "You can visit whenever," he says.

What is he, crazy? What does he think we are?

"You don't understand them. Nobody does. Except me."

We are not sure if this is true. The part about him understanding them. Perhaps. We know that we don't. The therapists say, "Give it time. Don't ask."

We ask them if they want meatloaf or roast chicken and they stare at us as if we have spoken Urdu. We show them photographs of the relatives who died while they were gone and find it disturbing that they nod, as if they understand, but show no grief. We stock the refrigerator with soda, though we know they should drink juice, and Gatorade, remembering how they used to gulp it down in great noisy swallows (and we scolded them for drinking right out of the bottle) after games of little league and soccer, though now they are happy to sit, listlessly, in front of the computer for hours, often wandering the house in the middle of the night. We ask them if their beds are comfortable enough, are they warm enough, are they cool enough, but we never ask them what happened because the therapists have told us not to. When we explain this to the famous lost boy (though why do we feel we have to explain ourselves to him? He can't even hold down a job at McDonald's) he says, "You don't ask, because you don't want to know."

We hate the famous lost boy, he sneers and ridicules and we do not want our sons to turn out like him. He is not a nice man. We just want him to go away, but he won't. Notoriously reclusive for years, he is now, suddenly, everywhere. Walking down Main Street. Hanging out at the coffee shops. Standing on the street corner, smoking. We are sorry to see that our boys seem to like him. Sometimes we find them, running together, like a wild pack. We call them home and they come back to us panting, tongues hanging out. They collapse on the couch or the floor and when they fall asleep they twitch and moan, cry and bark. We don't know what they dream about, though we think, often, they dream of running.

They run all the time now. In the morning they run down the stairs and around the kitchen table. We tell them to sit, or calm down, but it doesn't really work. Sometimes we open the door and they tear into the backyard. We have erected fences but they try to dig out, leaving potholes where tulips and tiger lilies and roses blossomed through all those years of our grief. We stand at the window wondering at the amazing fact of their tenacity in trying to escape us when (and this is public knowledge, much discussed and debated by newscasters and talk show hosts in those first heady weeks after they were found) they never tried to escape their beasts.

Sometimes we feel our neck hairs tingle and we find the lost boys staring at us like animals in a cage, frightened and wary, then they smile, and we smile in return, understanding that they will have these bad memories, these moments of fear.

The famous lost boy sighs, and right there, in the high school auditorium, lights a cigarette, which Hymral Waller, the school board president, rushes to tell him must be extinguished. "What?" the word sounds angry in the bite of microphone. "This?" Hymral's words drift from the floor, hollow, balloon-like, "fire," and "sorry." The famous lost boy drops the cigarette to the stage floor and stamps it out with the toe of his sneaker. We gasp at his impertinence and he squints at us.

"Okay. So, right. You're protecting your children by worrying about me and my friggin' cigarette?" He shakes his head, laughing a little jagged laugh, and then, without further comment, turns and walks out the fire exit door.

We should have just let him walk away. We should have gone home. But instead, we followed him, through the icy white streets of our town.

He walks down the cold sidewalk (neatly shoveled, only occasionally patched with ice) beneath the yellow street lamps, hunched in his flimsy jean jacket, hands thrust in his pocket, acrid smoke circles his head. We cannot see his face, but we imagine the nasty, derisive curl of his lips, the unruly eyebrows over slit eyes, the unshaved chin stubbled with small black hairs as though a miniscule forest fire raged there.

We walk on the cold, white sidewalks, beneath the blue moon and we breathe white puffs that disappear the way our sons did. We keep our distance. We are sure he does not realize we have followed him, until, suddenly, he leaps over the winter fence (meant to discourage errant sleigh riding from this dangerous hill) into the park. A shadow passes overhead, just for a second we are in darkness, and then, we are watching the shape of a lone wolf, its long tail down, its mouth open, tongue hanging out, loping across what, in spring, will be the baseball diamond. We all turn, suddenly, as if broken from some terrible spell, and, careful because of those occasional patches of ice, we run home where our lost boys wait for us. (Or so we like to think.) We find them sprawled, sleeping, on the kitchen floor, draped uncomfortably across the stairs, or curled, in odd positions, in the bathroom. We don't wake them. Any sleep they find is sorely needed and any interruption can keep them up for days, running in circles and howling at all hours. The doctors have advised us to give them sleeping pills but we are uncomfortable doing so; we understand that their captors often drugged them.

"It's not the same thing," the experts say.

Well, of course not. The experts are starting to get on our nerves.

And now, we realize, as we stand in the dark rooms of our miracle lives, we have been consulting the wrong professionals all along. We don't need psychologists, psychiatrists, medical doctors, or the famous lost boy. We need a hunter, someone who knows how to kill a wolf.

We find her on the internet and pool our resources to pay her airfare and lodging at the B&B downtown. We wish we had something more appropriate, fewer stuffed bears and fake flowers, more hunting lodge, but we don't.

When she arrives we are surprised at how petite she is, smaller than our boys, with an amazingly chipmunky voice and an odd xylophone laugh. She comes into the high school auditorium bearing the strong scent of the B&B roses soap, and we think we've been duped somehow, but, once we adjust our positions, craning our necks to see between shoulders, scooting over to the edge of the cold, hard chairs, adjusting to her unexpected size, she commands our attention.

"Now, wait a minute," she says, laughing (and we resist the temptation to cover our ears), "why are you all making this so complicated?"

We explain to her again how a werewolf roams amongst us, a monster! We shout and interrupt each other. We try to tell her how the werewolf was once one of our own. "We don't really want to hurt him," someone says. "We just want him gone."

At this she looks at us in such a way that we are all victims of her gaze. "Now wait a minute, why did you send for me? What am I doing here? Are you hunting or starting a zoo?"

There is a moment's silence. After all, a zoo might be nice, a perfect addition to our town, but from the back of the room, a voice cries out, "Hunting!" The cry is taken up by all of us. Our boys have been through enough. We will protect them at any cost.

The small, pink tip of her tongue protrudes between her pretty lips and she nods slowly, smiling. "He's not necessarily a werewolf. Not all men who turn into wolves are, uh, wait a minute. I'd like to get my fee now."

Duped! We've been duped after all. Suddenly it seems we have found ourselves in the middle of a bad joke, we'll pay her and she'll say something pithy and, all right, perhaps a little funny. Here's how you do it, she'll say and tell us something completely useless. We begin to argue this plan, what does she think we are, country hicks? Until finally she shrugs and nods at Hymral, who has volunteered to be her chauffer and local guide. He has reported that she asked him if there are any good vegetarian restaurants in the area, which we consider further evidence against her. A vegetarian hunter, who ever heard of such a thing? But when we confront her with all the evidence, her small frame, her flowered suitcases, her lack of weapons, she just shrugs. "What's going on here folks," she chirrups. "I've got ten jobs waiting for me right now and I ain't gonna stay another night, lovely as it is. If you want my expert guidance, you are going to have to pay me up front, 'cause the fact is, catching a wolf just ain't that hard, but I have to earn my living somehow."

"You gonna use your feminine wiles?"

She fixes such a look in the general direction of that question that we all shiver and step back as if separating ourselves from the inquisitor.

"I ain't no prostitute," she says, disgusted.

Well, what were we going to do? Consult more therapists with their various opinions and modalities? Call the sheriff who did everything he could to help us find our sons though none of it was enough and they came home only after a freak series of events? Pray, as we did for all those nights and all those days and all those hours upon minutes upon seconds when our sons were being torn apart? Or pay this little Goldilocks person to rid us of the danger that resided amongst us?

We pay her, of course.

He lives in a shack at the edge of town and he does not expect our arrival, though certainly he sees all our cars coming up the long, deserted road, headlights illuminating the talloned branches of trees and the swollen breasts of snow. Certainly he hears the car doors open and shut. We stand there whispering in the dark, observe the light go on in the small upstairs window and observe it go out again. We suspect he is watching us through the web of old lace curtain there. We feel horrible, just terrible about what we have come to do but we don't even consider not doing it. At last he opens his front door. He is wearing plaid flannel pajamas, boots, and that old jean jacket again, which, later, some of us recall, was the coat his parents bought him when he first came back, all those years ago. "What's up?" he says.

We don't look at each other, embarrassed, and then at last someone says, "Sorry Jamie, but you've got to come."

He nods, slowly. He turns to look back into his house, as though fondly, though later, when we went in there, we all agreed it was nothing to feel sentimental about, a beat-up couch, an ancient TV, a three legged kitchen table, and, both disturbing and proof of our right course, enormous stacks of children's books, fairy tales, and comics. To think he wanted us to send our boys here!

He shuts the door gently, thrusts his hands into his pockets, sniffs loudly. He works his mouth in an odd manner, the way boys do when they are trying not to cry.

He walked right to us, as though he had no say in the matter, as though he could not run, or shout, or lock himself in the house, he came to us like a friendly dog to kibble, like a child to sugar, he came to us as though there was no other possible destination. He didn't ask why or protest in any way. It was so strange. So inhuman.

She was giggling when she told us how to do it, as though it were all just a joke, but she was also counting a big stack of money at the time. "How you catch a wolf is you catch the man. This is something the French knew. You don't have to wait until he turns and his teeth are sharp and he has claws."

We live tidy lives; ice-free sidewalks, square green lawns, even our garages, so clean you could eat in them (and some of us do, using them as summer porches). We are not eager to do something so sloppy, but for our sons we make the sacrifice.

We cut and cut looking for the pelt.

"The wolf rests within," she said before she wiggled her red nail polished fingers at us and nodded for Hymral to take her to the airport.

We have grown sensitive now to the sound of screams. Our boys run through the town, playing the way boys do, shouting and what-not, but every once in a while they make a different sort of sound, blood-curdling, we always thought that was an expression, but when a man screams while being cut, his blood is dotted with bubbles as though it is going sour.

Once it was begun, it was impossible to stop.

"Wolf! Hair!" someone shouted holding up a thatch, which caused a tremendous amount of excitement until we realized it was scalp.

All we needed was the hair of the wolf trapped within the famous lost boy to redeem ourselves. There was no redemption.

Our boys slam the doors and kick the cats. We scold them. We love them. They look at us as though they suspect the very worst. They ask us about the famous lost boy and we say, "Don't ask" but they do, they ask again and again and again, they ask so much and so often that each of us, separately, reach a breaking point and turn on them, spitting the words out, the dangerous words, "What happened to you, while you were lost?"

They tell us. They tell us everything about the years upon months upon days upon hours upon minutes upon seconds. We sweat and cry. They gnash their teeth, pull their hair, scratch themselves incessantly. We try to hold them but they pull away. The sun sets and rises. We sleep to the drone of this terrible story and wake to another horrible chapter. We apologize for our need for sleep, but the recitation continues, uninterrupted, as if we are not the reason for it. We become disoriented, we have waking dreams, and in sleep we have death. Our boys change before us, from the lost sons we kissed on freckled noses to sharp toothed beasts. We shake our heads. We readjust.

And we know now that what we said for all those years was not just a promise, but a curse; we will always be searching for the boys that were taken from us. We will never find them, for they are lost, no grave to mark their passing and passage by which they can return, like dreams or the memory of sunshine in the dark. We fill their bowls with water, and they come in slobbering, tongues hanging out, collapsing on the floor or couch, shedding hair and skin and we would do anything for them, but still, some days, when the sun is bright or clear, you can find us staring out at the distant horizon. We have discovered that if we look long enough and hard enough we can see them again, our lost boys, their hair cuts ragged with youth, their smiles crooked. They are riding bicycles, jumping over rocks, playing with their friends, shoving hamburgers into their mouths, gulping soda, eating cake, running out the door, running down the sidewalk; the sun shining on them as if they were not just our sons, but sons of the gods and then, suddenly, we are brought back to the present, by that feeling at the back of our necks, and we turn to find them watching us with that look, that frightened, wary look of an animal caged by an unkind human. At moments like these, we smile, and sometimes, on good days, they smile back at us, revealing sharp white teeth in the tender red wounds of their mouths.

Traitor

(4th of July)

*A*LIKA WITH HER BRAIDS OF BELLS COMES WALK-ing down the street, chewing bubble gum and singing, "Who I am I'll always be, God bless you and God bless me, America, America, the land of the free!"

Rover says, "What's that song you're singing, Alika? That ain't no song."

Alika, only nine, ignores him the same way she's seen her mama ignore the comments of men when she walks with her to the bus stop or the Quickmart.

"Hey! I'm talking to you!" Rover says.

But Alika just walks on by and Rover just watches her pass. The girl is only nine and he is nearly twelve. He shakes his head and looks down the street in the other direction. Besides which, she is crazy. Shit, he spits at the sidewalk. Damn! He can't help it. He turns and watches her walking away, her braids jangling.

"America! America! Oh, I love America! My beautiful country, my own wonderful land, my homeland, America, loves me."

Alika's mom watches her and shakes her head. She drags her cigarette. Smoke swirls from her nostrils and mouth. Her fingers, with the long, green painted nails, tremble.

Alika sees her sitting there on the stoop. "Hi mama!" she calls.

The bells ring as she comes running down the walk. Running right toward her mama who sits there with smoke coming out of her ears and nose and mouth.

"Hey, baby," Alika's mother says. "Where you been?"

Alika stops in mid-running-step. Bells go *brrring, brrring*. She looks at her mama. Her mama looks at her. A truck passes. Fans and air-conditioners hum. Alika watches a bird fly into the branches of a tree, disappear into the green.

"Alika? Where you been honey?"

Alika shrugs. The bells jingle softly.

"Come here, child."

Alika walks over to her mama.

"Sit down." Her mama pats the step, right beside her.

Alika's butt touches her mother's hip. Alika's mother smells like cigarettes and orchid shampoo. She brings a trembling hand to her lips. Drags on the cigarette, turns to face Alika. Alika thinks she is the luckiest girl in America to have a mama so beautiful.

"You don't remember none of it?" she says.

Alika shakes her head. It always happens like this. Her mother puts an arm around her, pulls her tight. Alika's bells ring with a burst. "Good," her mama says. "Well, all right then. Good."

They sit there until their butts get sore and then they go inside. Alika blinks against the dark and she hums as she runs up the stairs. Her mother follows behind, so slow that Alika has to wait for her at the door. While she waits, Alika hops from one foot to another. The bells make a quick ring but Alika's mother says, "Shush, Alika, what did I tell you about making noise out here?"

Alika stands still while her mother unlocks the door. When she opens it, fans whirl the heat at them. Alika's mom says, "Shit." She closes the door. Locks it. Chains it. Alika says, "Won't do much good."

Alika's mother turns fast. "What?" she says with a sharp, mean voice.

Alika shrugs. *Brrring*. She spins away from her mother, singing, "Oh, America, my lovely home, America for me. America! America! The bloody and the free!"

"Alika!" her mother says.

Alika stops in mid-spin. Bells go *brrring brrring*, ring tingle tap. She keeps her arms spread out and her feet apart, her eyes focused on the light switch on the wall.

"I'm going into the room," Alika's mother says.

Alika knows what that means.

"I'll be out in a couple of hours. Your dinner is in the refrigerator. Nuke it for three minutes. And be careful when you take off the plastic wrap. Do you hear me Alika?"

Nod. (*Brrring.*)

"You're a good girl, Alika. Don't turn the TV too loud. Maybe we'll go get ice cream."

Alika's mother goes into the room. Alika resumes spinning.

The room is red, the color of resistance. It is stifling hot with all the shades pulled down. She's considered an air-conditioner but it seems selfish when the money could be better spent elsewhere. The resistance isn't about her being comfortable. She takes off her clothes and drops them to the floor. She walks across the room and flips on the radio. It cackles and whines as she flips through the noise. Damn station is always moving. It's never where it was the day before. Finally she finds it. Music comes into the room and fills it up. She is filled with music and red. She walks over to stare at the wall of the dead. She looks at each photograph and says, "I remember." They smile back at her in shades of black, white, and gray. Sometimes she is tempted to hurry through this part or just say a general "I remember" once to the entire wall. But she knows it isn't her thinking this. Resistance begins in the mind. I remember. She looks at each face. She remembers. It is never easy.

When that's finished she walks to the worktable. She sits down on the towel, folded across the chair. She looks at the small flag pasted on the wall there. The blue square filled with stars, the forbidden stripes of red and white. She nods. I remember. Then she flicks on the light and bends over her work.

Alika spins around six more times until she is so dizzy, she spins to the chair and plops down. When things fall back in order she looks at the closed door behind which her mother works. Red, Alika thinks and then, quickly shakes her belled braids to try not to think it again. Alika's mother doesn't know. Alika has been in the room. She's seen everything.

Hours later, after Alika has eaten the meatloaf and mashed potatoes and several peas; after the plate has been washed and dried and her milk poured down the drain, while she sits in the dim heat watching her favorite TV show, *This Is the Hour*, her mother comes out of the room, that strange expression on her face, her skin glossy with sweat, and says, "Hey honey, wanna go for ice cream?"

Alika looks at her and thinks, Traitor. She nods her head. Vigorously. The bells ring but the word stays in her mind.

It's a hot evening, so everybody is out. "Hi Alika!" they say. "Hi Pauline." Alika and her mother smile and wave, walking down the street. When somebody whistles they both pretend they don't hear and when they pass J.J. who sits on his stoop braiding his own baby girl's hair and he says, "My, my, my" they just ignore him too. Finally they get to the Quickmart.

"What flavors you got today?" says Alika's mother. Sometimes, when Mariel is working, they stand around and talk but this is some new girl they've never seen before. She says, "Today's flavors are vanilla, chocolate, and ice cream."

Alika's mother says, "Oh."

Alika says, "What's she mean ice cream? Of course the ice cream is flavored ice cream."

But Alika's mother doesn't pay much attention to her. She looks right at the girl and says, "So soon?" The girl says, "She's already nine. She's going to start remembering." Then she looks at Alika and says, "What flavor you want?"

Alika says, "You said vanilla, chocolate, and ice cream."

The girl smiles. Her teeth are extraordinarily white. Alika stares at them. "Did I say that?" the girl says. "I don't know what I was thinking. Flavors today are vanilla, chocolate, and hamburger."

"Hamburger?" Alika looks at her mother. This girl is nuts. But her mother is standing there just staring into space with this weird look on her face. "I'll have chocolate," Alika says. "I always take chocolate."

The girl nods. "Those sure are pretty braids," she says as she scoops chocolate ice cream into a cone.

"I only get one scoop," says Alika.

"Well today we're giving you three," says the girl with the brilliant white teeth.

Alika glances at her mother.

"Don't worry," the tooth girl says, "she already said it would be all right."

Alika doesn't remember that. She says, "I don't remember—"

But her mother interrupts her in that mean voice. "Oh Alika, you never remember anything. Take the ice cream. Just take it."

Alika looks at the girl. "That's not true," she says. "I remember some things."

The girl's eyes go wide.

Alika's mother grabs her by the wrist and pulls her, walking briskly out the door, Alika's bells ringing. "Mama," she says, "you forgot to pay that girl."

"It doesn't matter," Alika's mama says. "She's a friend of mine."

Alika turns but the girl no longer stands behind the counter. Some little kids run in and she can hear them shouting "Hey, anyone here?" Alika's mother lets go of her wrist but continues to walk briskly. Alika's bells ring. Her mama says, "You're more like me than anyone else."

Alika looks up at her beautiful mama and smiles.

But Alika's mama doesn't look at her. She stares straight ahead. She walks fast. Alika has to take little running steps to keep up. She can't hardly eat her ice cream. It drips over her fingers and wrist and down her arm. Alika licks her arm. "Mama," she says. Her mama doesn't pay her any mind. She just keeps walking, her legs like scissors, *pwish pwish pwish*. Her face like rock. Alika thinks, scissors, paper, rock. Her mama is scissors and rock. That makes Alika paper. "Hey mama," Alika says, "I'm paper." But her mother just keeps walking; *pwish pwish pwish*. Alika turns her wrist to lick her arm. The top two ice cream scoops fall to the sidewalk. "Shit," she says.

"What did you say?" the scissors stops and turns her rock face on Alika. "What did I just hear you say?"

"I'm sorry, mama."

"You're sorry?" The rock stands there. Waiting for an answer.

"Yes mama," Alika says in a tiny, papery voice.

The rock grabs Alika by the wrist, the one that is not dripping and sticky.

"Pauline, that girl of yours giving you trouble?"

The rock turns to face the voice but does not let go of Alika's wrist. "This little thing? She couldn't give trouble to a fly."

The ice cream in Alika's other hand drips down her arm, the cone collapsing. Alika doesn't know what to do so she drops it to the sidewalk.

The rock squeezes her wrist, "What did you do that for?"

"Ow, mama," Alika says, "you're hurting me." Her bells clack against each other.

"Stop it, Alika," says the rock. "I mean it now. Stop your twisting around this instant."

Alika stops.

The rock bends down, face close to Alika's. "I don't want you arguing or crying about some stupid ice cream cone. Do you hear me?"

Alika can see that the rock is crying. She nods. *Brrring. Brrring.*

The rock lets go of Alika's wrist. Alika has to run to keep up, her bells ringing. "Hey, Pauline. Hey, Alika." Scissors, rock, and paper. Paper covers rock. Scissors get old and rusty. Alika spreads her arms wide. She runs right past her mama. "Alika! Alika!" But she doesn't stop. She is a paper airplane now, or a paper bird. She can't stop. "Alika! Alika!" Her bells ring. "Alika!"

Her mother doesn't even scold her when she finds her waiting at the top of the stairs. She just says, "Time for bed now."

While Alika gets ready for bed Pauline goes into the red room. She takes the photographs down from the wall of the dead. She doesn't think about it. She just does it. She goes to the worktable, stares at it for a while and sighs. She'll have to stay up late to finish. What's she been doing anyway? With her time?

"Mama? I'm ready for my story."

She sets the stack of the dead on the worktable.

"Mama?"

"I'm coming!" she hollers. She doesn't even bother turning off the light. She'll be back in here soon enough, up half the night, getting everything ready.

What I'm going to tell you about tonight is ice. From before. When there were winters and all that. When I was a little girl I snuck in my daddy's truck one night. He and my brother, Jagger, were going ice fishing the next morning. They said girls couldn't come along. So I decided to just sneak a ride. I lay there, in the back of that truck all night. Let me tell you, it was cold. I had nothing but my clothes and a tarp to keep me warm. I know, you don't understand about cold. It was like being in the refrigerator, I guess. The freezer part, you know, 'cause that's where it's cold enough for ice. I lay there and looked at the stars. I tried to imagine a time like the one we live in right now. I tried to imagine being warm all over. I closed my eyes and pretended the sun was shining on my face. I guess it worked 'cause after a while I fell asleep.

I woke up when daddy and Jagger came out the door and walked over to the truck. I could hear their footsteps coming across the snow. It sounded like when you eat your cereal. They put the cooler in the back but they didn't see me hid under the tarp. They didn't discover me until we got to the lake. My daddy was mad, let me tell you. Jagger was too. But what were they going to do? Turn around? Daddy called my mama and told her what I did. I could hear her laughing. Jagger could hear her too. We stood there, by the side of the frozen lake and stared at each other. You never had a brother. You don't know what it's like. Daddy hung up the phone, put it in his pocket, and said, "Your mama is very disappointed in you." Then he told me all the rules. How I had to be quiet and stay out of the way. He gave me two big nails to carry in my pocket. They were supposed to help me grab hold of the ice if I fell in.

The lake was all frozen and pearly white at the edges. You could see the lights shining in half a dozen little shanties. Mama had made red and white curtains for ours.

Walking across that ice, the sky lit with stars, the faint glow of lights and murmur of voices coming from the shanties, I felt like I was in a beautiful world. Even the cold felt good out there. It filled my lungs. I pictured them, red and shaped like a broken heart.

When we get into our shanty, my dad lifts the wooden lid off the floor and Jagger starts chipping through the ice there, which was not so thick, my daddy said, since they'd been coming regularly. And then they sat on the benches and my dad popped open a beer. Jagger drank a hot chocolate out of the thermos my mama had prepared for him. He didn't offer to share and I didn't ask. It smelled bad in there, a combination of chocolate, beer, wet wool, and fish. So I asked my dad if it was all right that I went outside. He said just don't bother the other folk and don't wander too far from the ice shanties.

I walked across the ice, listening to the sound of my footsteps, the faint murmur of voices. The cold stopped hurting. I looked at all the trees surrounding the lake, a lot of pine, but also some bare oak and birch. I looked up at the stars and thought how they were like fish in the frozen sky.

Anyhow, that's how I came to be practically across the lake when I heard the first shouts and the next thing I know, ice shanties are tilting and everything is sinking. I hear this loud noise, and I look down. Right under me there is a crack, come all the way from where the ice shanties are sinking, to under my feet.

I finger the nails in my pocket though I am immediately doubtful that they will do me much good. At the same time, I start to step forward, because, even though I'm just a kid, I want to help. But when I lean forward the crack gets deeper. When I lean back to my original position the ice cracks again. Men are shouting and I even hear my daddy, calling Jagger's name. But there are only islands of ice between me and the drowning men.

I am maybe a half-mile away from the opposite shore. The ice in *that direction is fissured and cracked but appears to be basically intact, though even as I assess it, more fissures appear. What I have to do is walk away from my father and brother and all the drowning men. I was not stupid. I knew that it wouldn't take long for them to die, that it would take longer for me to walk across the ice. If I made it across. I would say that right at that moment, when I turned away from the men whose shouts were already growing weak, something inside of me turned into ice. It had to, don't you see? I decided to save the only person I could save, myself. I want you to understand, I never blamed myself for this decision. I don't regret it either._*

So, I clutch the nails in my fist and step forward. The ice cracks into a radiated circle like those drawings you used to make of the sun. What else can I do? I lift my foot to take another step. Right then a crow screams. I look up. It's as though that bird is shouting at me to stop. I bring my foot back. Slowly. When I set it down again, I can hear my breath let out. That's when I notice that there is no sound. Just my breath. There is no more shouting. I picture them under the ice, frozen. I picture their faces and the nails falling from ice fingers. It almost makes me want to give up. But instead I take a careful step and just when I feel that ice under me, I exhale, slowly. I want you to understand. I know now and I knew then, that ice doesn't breathe. But it was like I was breathing with the ice. I took the next step fast, and right beneath me the fissure separated. I had to forget about the dead, I had to stop my heart from beating so hard. I had to make myself still. Then, carefully, I lifted my leg. Slowly. Breathing like ice. I breathed like ice, even when I started sweating, and I kept breathing like ice, even when the tears came to my eyes. I did this until I got to the shore on the other side. Only then did I turn around and start bawling. There's a time for emotions, right?

Trucks and cars were parked all along the opposite shore. I could see our red Ford. But no one was standing there. Mist was rising off the lake. I ran and walked half way back before Mrs. Fando found me. She was driving out to scold her husband because he was late for work.

Folks treated me different after that. Everyone did. Everyone treated me the way Jagger used to, like I was too ugly to be alive or like I was some kind of a traitor. Even my own mother. Like I broke that ice under all those men and boys and murdered them myself. I tried to describe to them what happened and how I made it out by learning to breathe like ice but no one took me seriously. For a long time.

Then, when I was seventeen, this stranger came to town. People

noticed her because she dressed so well, drove a nice car and was ask-
ing about me. She had this old torn newspaper article from way back
and she said, "Is this you who survived that ice break up?" I said yes it
was. I thought she was maybe someone's girlfriend or grown daughter
coming to tell me she wished I had died and her man had lived. Folks
said stuff like that. But what she said was, "I think you need to come
with us." She was a recruiter. For the new army. You heard about that,
I'm sure.

Yep. That's what I want you to know about me, little girl. I never
told you this before. I want you to understand what I do isn't for
death. All those years ago I chose life, and I've been choosing it ever
since. I have some special skills is all. I can walk like water, for
instance; breathe like ice. I can build things. I have seen many people
die and I still choose to stay alive. Those are qualities they look for in
soldiers.

What I want you to understand is that all the time since then, I
think I turned partly into ice. Until you came along. You came along
and thawed me out, I guess. It's like that feeling I had, when I was
walking out on the ice and I thought the world was a beautiful place.
I have that feeling again with you. I couldn't love you more if you were
my natural born daughter. Do you understand what I'm trying to say?
I bet none of this makes any sense to you at all.

Pauline leans down and kisses Alika's forehead. Alika rolls over, her
bells go *brrring*. "Damn bells," says Pauline. She shuts off the light.
Walks out of the room.

Alika opens her eyes. She sits up. Slowly. Alika knows how to
move so carefully that the bells don't ring. Alika grabs the end of
one of the braids. Slowly, she twists the bell off. It doesn't make a
sound. What do they think? She's stupid or something?

She has to keep herself awake for a long time. Her mama is in
the forbidden room almost all night long. She keeps herself from
falling asleep by remembering the pictures she saw on that wall.
All those photographs of smiling children wearing backpacks. My
sisters, Alika thinks.

It is already light out when she hears the forbidden door open
and shut, her mother walking across the apartment to her own bedroom. When Alika leaves her room, she doesn't make a sound. The
bells remain on her pillow. The first thing she notices is the smell
of paint. The forbidden room is no longer red. It is white. All the
pictures are gone. The worktable is folded up against the wall,

beside the bookshelf. Alika can just barely see where the flag had been pasted. The paint there is a little rougher. But the flag is gone. Next to the door is her mama's suitcase, and a backpack and a camera. Alika opens up the backpack. Very carefully. She sighs at the wires. "Be one with the backpack," she says to herself. "Breathe like ice," she rolls her eyes.

By the time she leaves the room, it is bright out. She just gets the last bell in her hair when her mama comes in and says, "Get up now honey. Today is going to be a special day. I got you a new backpack."

Alika gets up. Her bells go *brrring*. She goes to the bathroom. She can just see the top of her eyes, in the mirror over the sink. She changes into her yellow butterfly top and her white shorts. It's already hot. She eats a big bowl of cereal, sitting alone at the kitchen table. Her bells make little bursts of sound that accompany her chewing, which is like the sound of footsteps walking across snow her mama said. Sun pours through the white curtain on the window over the sink. After she brushes her teeth she stands in the kitchen and sings, "America, America, how I love you true. America, America the white stars and the blue."

"Ok, child. Come here now." Alika's mama stands in the forbidden room. The door is wide open. "Look what I have for you. A new backpack!"

Alika spins. Her bells go *brrring, brrring, brrring*.

"Alika! Alika!" Her mama says, "Stop spinning now."

Alika stops spinning.

"Let me put this on you."

Alika looks up at her mama, the most beautiful mother in the world. "There's something you should know about me," Alika says.

Alika's mama sighs. She keeps the backpack held out in front of her. "What is it Alika?"

"I'm not stupid."

Alika's mama nods. "Of course you're not," she says. "You're my little girl, aren't you? Now come here and put this thing on."

After Alika's mama buckles the backpack on her she locks it with a little key and puts the key into her own pocket.

"Don't I need that?" Alika says.

"No you don't," her mama says. "Today we're doing things a little different. You get to keep this backpack. Not like the others that you had to drop off somewhere. This one is for you to keep. Your teacher will unlock it when you get to school. I gave her the extra key, okay? Now come over here. I want to take your picture."

Alika follows the map her mother drew. "You have to take a different way to school today," she said. Her hands were shaking when she drew it. Alika follows the wavy lines, down Arlington Avenue past the drugstore and video place, turning right on Market Street. Alika's bells ring once or twice, but her step is slow. The backpack is heavy. She has to concentrate on these new directions.

"Hey, where you going?" Rover stands right in front of her. "Ain't you supposed to be at school?"

Alika shrugs, "I'm taking a different way."

Rover shakes his head. "Are you crazy, girl? This is no place for you. Don't you know you are heading right into a war zone?"

Alika smirks, "This is what my mama wants me to do."

"You better turn around right now," Rover says. "Less your mama wants you dead."

Alika doesn't mind turning around, because suddenly she re-members everything. She walks back home. She doesn't feel like singing. When she gets to their building she looks up and sees that the windows are all open, even the windows in the forbidden room. She walks up the hot, dark stairs. She gets there just as her mama is stepping into the hallway with her suitcase.

"Hi mama," Alika says.

Alika's mama turns, her face rock, liquid, rock. "What are you doing here?"

"I forgot to hug you goodbye," Alika says.

Her mama steps back. Then, with swift precision, she steps for-ward as she reaches into her pocket, pulls out the little key, and unlocks Alika's backpack. She runs across the apartment and throws the backpack out the window. Even before it hits the ground she is wrapped around Alika. They are crouched, in tight embrace. After a few seconds, she lets go.

"You all right, mama?" Alika says.

She nods, slowly.

"I don't know what to tell my teacher about my books. What should I tell her, mama?"

Pauline gets up, walks across the apartment and leans out the window. Scattered on the ground below is the backpack, and several large books. She is shaking her head, trying to understand what has happened, when she sees Alika, with her belled braids, skipping down the steps, walking wide around the scattered contents of her backpack. Then, with a quick look up at the window, Alika breaks into a run, her bells ringing.

Pauline turns, fast. She looks at her suitcase in the hallway, runs to it, thinking (Alika?) she will toss it out the window, but she is not fast enough.

All the dead children are reaching for her. She tries to exhale, but there is no breath. She sinks where she steps, grabbed by the tiny, bony fingers pulling her into the frozen depths. Rusty nails clutched in the ice children's hands pierce her skin. How quiet it is, the white silence punctuated only by the distant sound of bells. Why, that's Alika, she thinks, that's my girl. Astonished. Proud. Angry.

Alika stands, gazing at the bombed building, feeling certain there is something she has forgotten. An annoying fly, which has been circling her head, lands on her arm and Alika soundlessly slaps it, leaving a bright red mark on her skin, which she rubs until the burning stops. Then she turns and skips down the walk, in this mysterious silent world, even her belled braids, gone suddenly mute. An ambulance speeds past, the red light flashing, but making no sound and Alika suddenly understands what has occurred. She has fallen into the frozen world. Surely her mother will come for her, surely her brave mother will risk everything to save her. Alika looks up at the white sky, reaches her arms to the white sun, bawling like a baby, waiting for her beautiful mother to come.

Was She Wicked?
Was She Good?

(Summer – anniversary)

SHE LEAVES THE SMALL CREATURES IN TOR-
tured juxtapositions. Her mother and I find them on the
porch steps, in the garden, drowning in small puddles, the green
hose dripping water from the copper nozzle, guilty as blood. For a
few weeks we are able to believe that these tragedies have nothing to
do with our little girl whose smile breaks each morning like the sun.
We scrape them up, gently, with the edge of leaves or blades of grass
(once I cut one in half that way, a horrible accident and it bled
while Sheilah laughed, I thought at some imaginary play) but we
save none. Sometimes, we have to take them out of their misery, the
slow agony of dying they suffer, we step on them, hard, and later
scrape their squashed remains from the soles of our shoes.

It has been a long, hot summer. The flowers wither on exhausted stems. We almost regret our stance against air conditioning.
We place fans throughout the house, the hum is as annoying as the
insidious hum of hornets that occasionally circle over us in the
garden, like a threat.

Sheilah runs through the summer days in her nightgown, pale
pink and ethereal, her white limbs and moon white face protected
by slatherings of coconut scented sunscreen. At night, when she
finally falls asleep, tiny beads of sweat dotting her pink lips, heat

emanates from her blonde curls as if she, herself, were a season.

Had there been earlier signs that we ignored? Certainly, we tried to believe it was all accident and coincidence until, at last, she brought her game into the house. We found them in gruesome cups of strange concoctions in the kitchen, combinations of balsamic vinegar, Worcester Sauce, and food coloring, their tiny bodies floating in the noxious liquid, we found them in the ice cubes, fingers splayed against their frozen death, finally we find them in Sheilah's bedroom, pinned alive to a bulletin board that displays her kindergarten graduation certificate, her blue ribbon for good citizenship, and a drawing of a horse. They are screaming but they are beyond being saved, we unpin them and hit them with the bottom of our shoes, feeling worst about the one who survived our repeated attempts at mercy killing only to die in agony. From this upstairs window we watch Sheilah. She is, once again, dressed in the silky pink sleeveless nightgown, sitting on a quilt under the oak tree. One second we are looking down at the golden haloed head of our child, her murmured voice rising up to us, pretty as the cardinal's morning song, and the next, we are running out of the room, down the wooden stairs, through the meditation room, into the kitchen (with its bright windows and spider plants) down the concrete steps lined with terra cotta pots filled with geraniums, awkwardly running across the lawn to Sheilah who sits on the old quilt beneath the ancient tree, plucking wings and severing limbs, the damaged and wounded writhing in agony while she sings.

With a moan, Anne scoops Sheilah up and runs back into the house, as though escaping a tornado, which leaves me to take care of the mess. I apologize to each and every one. I beg forgiveness. Their eyes lock into mine, infinitesimal eyes filled with the infinite suffering my daughter has caused. Later, when I go inside, I find Anne closing all the windows. "What are you doing?" I ask. "Isn't this why we moved to the country? It'll be a hundred degrees in here."

She looks at me with bright eyes, as though she suffers a fever. "They aren't going to let her get away with this," she says. "You know they won't."

"You're right," I nod. "We need to punish her."

Anne turns from the closed window, the air around us charged, like the feeling before a storm. "What are you saying?"

I step toward her but stop when I see the stone of her face, once beautiful, now set into the hard lines first etched three years ago. "Maybe we should reconsider. Maybe a little punishment—"

She turns away from me, she whirls out of the room. I stand there and listen to the sound of windows being slammed shut. This is a difficult time for all of us. Anne makes jewelry in the basement studio, which Sheilah is forbidden to enter, while I work on my second book (*The Possibilities for Enchantment in a World at War with the Self, the Other, and the Infinite*) in my upstairs office, also forbidden. Sheilah follows this rule so completely that, one morning, I find her lying curled against the door, like a good dog.

"Why don't you go play?"

She looks up at me, her eyes bright and wide as pennies. "You mean outside?" she asks.

I shake my head. Sadly. "No, Sheilah, not outside."

She purses her lips into rosebud shape. "I wanna go outside."

Every time she mentions the outdoors I picture the little bodies, the dark eyes, the strange combination of her singing and their small screams. "We've already talked about this, Sheilah. No."

"Why not why not why not?" she wails.

"You know why," I say, and am surprised by how mean I sound. She stops her whining. She stares at me. I can't tell if her expression is one of insolence, or horror. I step around her, carefully shutting the door behind me. My office window overlooks the backyard. I press up on the sash, hard. These are old windows, with screens and stormers that we change each spring and fall, a massive undertaking we had not considered when we bought the place, frantic to make our escape. I breathe in the scent of dirt, roses, leaves, grass, the green, loamy scent of summer, but my reverie is interrupted by droning, low and near. Hanging from the eave, like some dark tumor, is the hornet's nest.

I am both repelled and fascinated by the hornets, their golden wings quivering as they work their way around the orb. Sheilah is no longer screaming, perhaps she's gone to bother Anne, or maybe she's actually playing with her crystals or her chemistry set. I breathe in until I become restless and can't stand still any longer, then I pull down the sash. The effect is immediate; stifled in my own home. I inspect the room carefully, checking the corners, the ceiling, the hiding places behind the furniture.

We are striving for something like normal. The thought of having a "normal" child would once have struck us as a failing. Now it is our hope. The honey butter melts across the biscuits and we wash our hands under the tap as we stare out the closed window, remembering how we used to lick each other's sticky fingers. When she comes into the kitchen, wearing that nightgown, her hair a wild cloud around her sleep-pink face, we greet her joyfully. She pushes us away with her tiny, dangerous hands. She sighs like an old woman. She demands white bread (who knows where she was introduced to this vile concoction) toasted and slathered with sugary peanut butter. She chews with her mouth open, her pearled teeth coated with oily brown, and squints at us. "I wanna go outside."

We shake our heads.

"Why not why not why not," she cries and flings the toast to the floor, where she follows it in a spectacular display of temper. "Why not why not why not?" We sit in the rays of morning sun, sealed in with her screams and the heavy moaning heat, and it does not escape me that, in a way, we have become her victims.

Many nights, after Sheliah falls asleep in mid-protest, Anne goes outside, only to return streaked with dirt and grass, her blue eyes bereft of even the memory of joy. She does not invite me to join her, but one night I follow, allowing myself the freedom we must deny our daughter. Anne sits in the garden on a rock large enough, just barely, for one. She does not acknowledge me. Once my eyes adjust, I see what she has done. Miniature tombstones stand in neat rows, flowers in acorn cups arranged before them. I glance at Anne, then lean closer. Each stone is carved with a symbol; a star, a moon, a little shoe, a feather, a clock.

"I didn't know their names."

"Anne, listen, we—"

"Don't. Don't try to make this right with words."

What else do I have? I stand there at the foot of the fairies' graveyard for a long time, hoping that Anne will speak, but she doesn't. Finally, I turn around and walk back inside, immediately assaulted by the hot air, the droning fans, and Sheilah's screams, wild with terror. I take the steps, two at a time, slipping on the braided rug, pushing against the floor as I call, "I'm coming! Daddy's here."

She is sitting in bed, tears streaming down her face, her mouth open, her hair blowing up and back as though she is possessed, but before I can take her in my arms, Anne swoops past. She turns to me, her eyes wide, her own hair blowing in the hot fan wind. "What happened?"

I shrug. Anne frowns as if I have failed her with this answer. (I have failed her with this answer.) She is holding Sheilah, swaying side to side. The room is stifling, too hot with its shut windows, and too stuffy with a vague, sour odor. Suddenly, I feel nauseous. I step into the hall to catch my breath. Anne follows. "You can't do this right now. You have to make sure the room is safe." Reluctantly, I step back into the bedroom. The windows are closed and locked. I check behind the door, look in the closet. I even look under the bed. Finished with my search, I follow the sound of Anne's cooing, downstairs into the living room, where the standing fan gently hums, its great unwieldy head turning slowly in repeated surveyance of mother and daughter sitting in the flowered chair. The windows are locked against the black night as though it is something that will creep in and destroy us if we give it any quarter.

"Can you tell me what frightened you? Can you tell Daddy?"

Sheilah sits in her mother's lap, her curls damp at the back of her neck. She glances up at me with her copper eyes and I see in them, for just a moment, the look of murder before her long lashes flutter down. "Wings," she says.

"Wings?" her mother and I repeat.

She nods, and, sniffling loudly wraps her small arms around Anne's neck. The fan blows over us while Anne gently rocks. "I told you they would come after her."

"It was just a dream. A nightmare. Kids—"

"No. It was them. Do something, Michael."

"We need to punish her."

Anne holds Sheilah closer, as if I have suggested releasing her into the dark yard where those who seek revenge could have their way.

"We've already discussed this."

"I'm not saying we do anything corporal, I'm just saying that we need to show her that what she's doing is wrong. They won't bother her if she stops hurting them."

"No."

"Anne, listen to me—"

"Why should I? Do you listen to me? Do you ever listen to me? I told you we should have taken her to a different doctor. I told you he didn't understand people like us. I told you—"

"When? No. You didn't. You never said . . ."

Sheilah stirs against Anne, turning her head to reveal her profile, damp with sweat, wet curls plastered against her cheek.

"We're not going to punish her," Anne hisses. "She's already been through enough." She scoots to the edge of the chair and stands up, her eyes sharp on my face. "You're obsessed with vengeance."

"Don't be ridiculous."

"Ridiculous," she says as she passes me. It's only when I hear the creaking of the stairs that I realize she was calling me a name.

The fissures have formed beneath us, and I am not so far gone that I don't recognize we are falling. I stand there, I don't know for how long, as if any movement would collapse the careful arc that keeps us suspended. The fan drones, how I hate that sound.

Sheilah is sleeping with Anne in our bed. I try to move quietly, but they both stir when I crawl in beside them. For a while I just lay there, watching them breathe.

Bright light streams through the lace curtains of the humming room, and I awake to the sound of Anne weeping. I wrap her in my arms. She tries to explain but the words are swallowed by her tears. I pat her gently on the back. Over her shoulder I see Sheilah standing in the doorway in her favorite nightgown. She watches with a cold, calculated expression, holding in her dimpled fingers a fairy, so small it is almost invisible. Careful to cover the tiny mouth with her pinky she pulls one wing off the poor creature, and then the other. I take a deep breath and hold Anne closer.

We've had this problem with windows before, when we lived in the city. I begged Anne to lock them at night but she "couldn't feel closed in" and "had to have fresh air." Eventually, I had boards cut to size so that the windows could be left partially open, but safe. She used them for a while, but then one night she "forgot," or so she's always said, and I never had the heart to confront her about it. Whether she forgot to close the windows or not, her intention had been to let in the breeze, not the night creatures, with their masks and guns.

"This happens every year. It's like we're all stuck in some kind of cycle."

"We're not stuck," she says. "We moved. That's one thing. I'm making jewelry again. You're working on your book. We are making progress. Give me some credit."

Over Anne's shoulder, Sheilah pulls one leg off the poor fairy and then the other.

"No."

Anne pulls away from me, her face hard. Behind her Sheilah tosses wings, legs, and corpse to the floor, then walks down the hall, humming.

"I mean, you're right. Of course. We're not stuck, we're just, this is just a hard time of year for us and I was thinking that it might be nice for you to take a break."

"But how can I leave her, so close to the anniversary?"

"She'll be fine. She'll be with me. Besides, we don't even know if she remembers anything about that night."

Anne shakes her head. "It doesn't matter whether she remembers," she says. "What do you think this is all about?"

It is disturbing, how eagerly she leaves. Sheilah and I wave from the open doorway, the scent of summer dying in the morning air, the brown lilacs withered on the bush, the squirrels scampering wildly through the yard, which is overgrown and dried out. Anne waves from the open car window, the graceful arc of her hand the last we see of her as she turns the corner. Sheilah starts walking across the porch, she turns and looks at me, wonder and fear in her small face. I nod. She breaks into that brilliant smile, and with a shout, runs free, a wild thing released. Later, I lay the quilt under the tree, and bring out a thermos of lemonade, and peanut butter and jelly sandwiches. She gulps the lemonade, and tears into the sandwich. With her mouth full, she looks up at me, smiles, and plants peanut butter kisses all over my face.

She plays outside all day, and into the evening. When I call her in, she comes, tired and happy. She sits at the kitchen table and stares at the macaroni and cheese, her favorite food, but she cannot eat, instead she slumps forward, falling asleep, right there at the table. I carry her upstairs, and put her to bed in the clothes she played in.

I go from room to room opening all the windows and turning off the fans. The damp night air smells sweet, and reminds me of the scented candle Anne had in her bedroom when we first met. I stand at the open window of my office, breathing in the memory of those wild nights of limb and skin, when we discovered each other so thoroughly it was as though we were created by touch. I lean into the screen and it pops. I press just a little harder, it comes loose but doesn't fall. I pound it with my fist, remembering, as I do, how I hammered the corners to make it secure. It's an old house and we often found the screens fallen or dangling.

"What are you doing?"

"Go back to bed, Sheilah. I'm fixing something."

"I'm thirsty."

"Go back to bed. I'll bring you a glass of water as soon as I'm finished."

She looks at the open window. "Mommy's going to be mad."

"Yes, she is. If she calls and finds out that you are still awake she's going to be very angry at you."

Sheilah's face contorts. I have confused her, taken advantage of her logic skills, rooted, as they are, in her six-year-old mind. "Go on now."

Her eyes narrow as she glances from me to the window and back again.

"Go on."

She shuffles out of the room, like a little old lady, weary with the wrongs of the world.

I hit the screen three more times, wincing with pain until, at last, it loosens, only to dangle by the bottom left corner. The hornet nest is silent, two hornets, the night guards, cling to its side.

"Daddy? I'm ready for my water now."

It takes both hands to wrench the thing free. My knuckles are bleeding.

"Daddy!"

Finally it comes undone. I shove it away, approximating a throw, it crashes to the ground, followed by a sound of brush scattered, twigs broken. I have frightened some creature down there, a deer, or perhaps something more dangerous.

"Daddy!"

When I walk into Sheilah's room her eyes widen. I hand her the glass of water. "Drink it," I say, and then I say it again, in a gentle tone. "Drink it, honey."

She shakes her head vigorously. "Don't wanna," she says.

I snatch the glass from her. Water slops out. "Go to sleep, now." I lay my hand on her head, bend down to kiss her. As I leave the room I prop open the door with the big book of Grimm, the one with the fake gold edging on all the pages.

Downstairs, the rich scented summer air flows through the rooms. I sit in the flowered chair, sipping last year's clover wine. It was on just such a night as this that we were ruined. I fall asleep remembering the screams, the terror, the open windows. Screams. I wake to her screams, my heart pounding like a trapped creature. She screams, and I run through the rooms brightened by morning sun. "I'm coming," I shout, "Daddy's here." I race up the stairs and do not hesitate as I approach her room, abuzz with dark noise and screams. She is sitting up, covered by them as if she were made of honey, their golden wings trembling. I can see her halo of hair, though some alight there as well, her mouth, open but blackened by their writhing. I grab a blanket and swing it but this only heightens their attack, she screams and they sting me without mercy.

"Daddy's here, Daddy's here," I say even as I run out of the room, down the sunlit hall (but wait, what was that scurrying to hide in the corner) to the bathroom where I draw the water, which comes out languidly. I run back to the room, "Daddy's here," I say over and over again, wrapping her in the blanket. She screams at their new assault. Through the blanket I feel their squirming, their soft bodies, their stings. I rush down the hall to the bathroom, set her in the bath, she screams. I tear the blanket off, it is alive with wings, I press it, and her under the water, releasing her just long enough for screams and breath before I hold her under again. They fly at me, as if they understand what I am doing. The water is black with them. She struggles against my grasp, her mouth wide with screams, I dunk her one more time, then I carry her, heavy and wet and screaming, down the hall, slipping but not falling, down the stairs (and there, what was that behind the potted plant, and what just flew overhead) I hold her close even as they continue to sting. I grab my car keys from the kitchen counter, I run down the crooked path. They follow us, stinging again and again, she screams and I scream too as I set her in the car. A few of them follow, but only a few. I kill them with a rolled up atlas. At least now she understands, I think, now she knows not to harm a creature with wings.

Although it is late fall we are making up for lost time and spend much of our evenings outdoors. Anne is sitting in the garden, painting a small portrait of a fairy. She has never accused me of doing anything more than opening all the windows on a hot summer night. Why has she stayed, knowing even this? Well, why did I stay three years ago? I like to think it is love, this tendency to believe in each other's innocence, but maybe it's something else. I sit here, on the porch, writing in this notebook, sipping dandelion wine we bought from an old German fellow at the Farmer's Market. Sheilah sits on the blanket beneath the oak. She is almost entirely recovered though she moves strangely at times, with an odd, careful slowness that you would expect from someone wounded, or very old. They had to shave her head. Her hair has grown in strange, bristly and sharp. The doctors say that it will likely fall out, this sort of thing happens sometimes as a result of trauma, and already there are a few patches of soft hair coming in behind her ears, no longer blonde, but pure white. She sits on her quilt, dressed in jeans and a cotton sweater, playing some sort of game with fallen leaves, they are scolding each other, their leafy voices brittle.

As the amber evening closes in around us, and the night fairies come out, carrying their tiny lanterns, whispering their dark thoughts, Sheilah continues playing, even when a parade of them crosses the patches of her blanket, even when several fly right past her, she pays them no mind at all. Anne and I have begun to suspect she no longer sees them, which is sad in a way, but given the choices we had, and what life made of us, we think we have done well by Sheilah. Now that we have a normal child, she will be safe in her normal world, and we will be safe in ours. We hope, we dream, we believe.

You Have Never Been Here

(Halloween)

*Y*OU ARE ON THE TRAIN, CONSIDERING THE TIPS
of your clean fingers against the dirty glass through which
you watch the small shapes of bodies, the silhouettes on the street,
hurrying past in long coats, clutching briefcases, or there, that one
in jeans and a sweater, hunched shoulders beneath a backpack. Any
one of them would do. You resist the temptation to look at faces
because faces can be deceiving, faces can make you think there is
such a thing as a person, the mass illusion everyone falls for until
they learn what you have come to learn (too young, you are too
young for such terrible knowledge) that there are no people here,
there are only bodies, separate from what they contain, husks.
Useless, eventually.

Yours is useless now, or most nearly, though it doesn't feel like it,
the Doctors have assured you it is true, your body is moving toward
disintegration even as it sits here with you on this train, behaving
normally, moving with your breath and at your will. See, there, you
move your hand against the glass *because you decided to*, you wipe
your eyes *because you wanted to* (and your eyes are tired, but that is
not a matter of alarm, you were up all night, so of course your eyes
are tired), you sink further into the vague cushion of the seat, you do
that, or your body does that because you tell it to, so no wonder you

fell for the illusion of a body that belongs to you, no wonder you believed it, no wonder you loved it. Oh! How you love it still!

You look out the dirty window, blinking away the tears that have so quickly formed. You are leaving the city now. What city is this anyways? You have lost track. Later, you'll ask someone. Where are we? And, not understanding, he will say, We're on a train. The edge of the city is littered with trash, the sharp scrawls of bright graffiti, houses with tiny lawns, laundry hanging on the line, Christmas lights strung across a porch, though it is too late or too early for that. You close your eyes. Let me sleep, you say to your body. Right? But no, you must admit, your body needs sleep so the body's eyes close and it swallows you, the way it's always done, the body says sleep so you sleep, just like that, you are gone.

The hospital, the Doctors say, has been here for a long time. It's one of those wonderful secrets, like the tiny, still undiscovered insects, like several sea creatures, like the rumored, but not proven aliens from other planets, like angels, like God, the hospital is one of the mysteries, something many people know for a fact which others discount variously as illusion, indigestion, dreams, spiritual hunger, fantasy, science fiction, rumor, lies, insanity.

It is made of brick and stucco (architecturally unfortunate but a reflection of the need for expansion) and it has a staff of a hundred and fifty. With a population that large, the rotating roster of patients, the salespeople who wander in offering medical supplies (not understanding what they do to sick bodies here), the food vendors, the occasional lost traveler (never returned to the world in quite the same way) it is remarkable that the hospital remains a secret.

The patients come to the auditorium for an orientation. Some, naively, bring suitcases. The Doctors do nothing about this. There is a point in the process when the familiar clothes are discarded. It's not the same for everyone and the Doctors have learned that it's best not to rush things.

The Doctors appear to be watching with bored disinterest as the patients file in. But this is not, in fact, the case. The Doctors are taking notes. They don't need pen and paper to do this, of course. They have developed their skills of observation quite keenly. They remember you, when you come in, skulking at the back of the room, like the teenager you so recently were, sliding into the auditorium chair, and crouching over as though afraid you will be singled out as being too young to be here, but that is ridiculous as there are several children in the group flocking around that lady, the one with orangey-red hair and the red and yellow kimono draped loosely over purple blouse and pants, a long, purple scarf wrapped around her bloody neck. For some reason she is laughing while everyone else is solemn, even the Doctors standing there in their white lab coats, their eyes hooded as though supremely bored. (Though you are wrong about this. The Doctors are never bored.)

The Doctors introduce themselves. They hope everyone had a good trip. They know there is some confusion and fear. That's okay. It's normal. It's okay if there is none as well. That's normal too. All the feelings are normal and no one should worry about them.

The Doctors explain that the doors are locked but anyone can leave at any time. Just ring the bell and we will let you out.

The orangey-red-haired lady with the bloody neck raises her hand and the Doctors nod. You have to lean over to hear her raspy voice.

How often does that happen? How often does someone leave without going through with the procedure?

The Doctors confer amongst themselves. Never, they say in unison. It never happens.

The Doctors pass out room assignments and a folder that contains information about the dining hall (open for breakfast from six to nine, lunch from eleven-thirty to two, and dinner from five-thirty to eight), the swimming pool (towels and suits provided), the chapel (various denominational services offered throughout the week). The folder contains a map that designates these areas as well as the site of the operating rooms (marked with giant red smiley faces) and the areas that house the Doctors, which are marked Private, though, the Doctors say, if there is an emergency it would be all right to enter the halls which, on the map, have thick, black lines across them.

Finally, the Doctors say, there is an assignment. This is the first step in the operation. The procedure cannot go any further until the first step is complete. The Doctors glance at each other and nod. Don't be afraid, they say. Things are different here. Everything will be all right, and then, as an afterthought, almost as though they'd forgotten what they had been talking about, they say, find someone to love.

The auditorium is suddenly weirdly silent. As though the bodies have forgotten to breathe.

It's simple really, the Doctors say. Love someone.

You look around. Are they nuts?

At the front of the room the Doctors are laughing. No one is sure what to do. You see everyone looking around nervously, you catch a couple people looking at you but they look away immediately. You're not insulted by this. You expect it even.

The bloody neck lady raises her hand again. The Doctors nod.

Just one? she rasps.

The Doctors say, no, no, it can be one. It can be many.

And what happens next?

The Doctors shrug. They are organizing their papers and making their own plans for the evening. Apparently the meeting is over. Several patients stand, staring at the map in their hands, squinting at the exit signs.

Excuse me? the lady says again.

You can't decide if you admire her persistence or find it annoying but you wish she'd do something about her throat, suck on a lozenge maybe.

The Doctors nod.

After we find people to love, what do we do?

The Doctors shrug. Love them, they say.

This seems to make perfect sense to her. She stands up. The children stand too. They leave in a group, like a kindergarten class, you think. Actually, you kind of want to go with them. But you can't. You look at the map in your hand. You find your exit and you walk toward it, only glancing up to avoid colliding with the others. Love someone? What's this shit all about? Love someone? Let someone love me, you think, angry at first and then, sadly. Let someone love me.

The bodies move down the long hallways, weaving around each other, pausing at doors with numbers and pictures on them. (Later, you find out the pictures are for the children who are too young to know their numbers). The bodies open unlocked doors and the bodies see pleasant rooms painted yellow, wallpapered with roses, cream colored, pale blue, soft green, furnished with antiques and wicker. The bodies walk to the locked windows and stare out at the courtyard, a pleasant scene of grass and fountain, flowering fruit trees. The bodies open the closets filled with an odd assortment of clothes, plaid pants, striped shirts, flowery dresses, A-line skirts, knickers, hand-knit sweaters, and raincoats, all in various sizes. The bodies flick on the bathroom lights, which reveal toilets, sinks, tubs, and showers, large white towels hanging from heated towel racks.

The bodies look at the beds with feather pillows and down com-
forters. The bodies breathe, the bodies breathe, the bodies breathe.
The bodies are perfect breathers. For now.

What if this is the strangest dream you ever had? What if none of
this is true? The Doctors have not told you that your body has its
own agenda, your mother has not held your hand and squeezed it
tight, tears in her eyes, your father has never hugged you as though
he thought you might suddenly float away, your hair has not fallen
out, your skin become so dry it hurts, your swallowing blistered?
What if all of this is only that you are having a strange dream? What
if you aren't sick at all, only sleeping?

The Doctors eat pepperoni and discuss astronomy, bowling, lipo-
suction, and who has been seen kissing when someone's spouse was
away at a seminar. The Doctors drink red wine and eat pheasant
stuffed with gooseberries and cornbread, a side of golden-hashed
potatoes, green beans with slivered almonds and too much butter.
They discuss spectral philosophy, spiritual monasticy, and biological
relativism. They lean back in their chairs and loosen belts and buttons surreptitiously, burping behind hands or into napkins. Dessert
is served on pink plates, chocolate cake with raspberry filling and
chocolate frosting. Coffee and tea is served in individual pots. The
Doctors say they couldn't possibly and then they pick up thin, silver
forks and slice into the cake, the raspberry gooing out. "What do
you think they are doing now?" someone says. "Oh, they are crying,"
several of the Doctors respond. The Doctors nod their knowledgeable heads. Yes. On this first night, the bodies are crying.

That first night is followed by other days and other nights and all
around you life happens. There are barbecues, movies, tea parties,
and dances. The scent of seared meat, popcorn, and Earl Grey tea
wafts through the halls. You are amazed to observe everyone behaving as if this is all just the usual thing. Even the children, sickly
pale, more ears and feet than anything, seem to have relaxed into
the spirit of their surroundings. They ride bicycles, scooters, and
skateboards down the hall, shouting, Excuse me, mister! Excuse
me! You can never walk in a line from one end to the other and this
is how, distracted and mumbling under your breath, you come face
to face with the strange orange-haired woman. She no longer wears
the kimono but the scarf remains around her throat, bloodied pur-

ple silk trailing down a black, white, and yellow daisy dress. Her head, topped with a paper crown, is haloed with orange feathers, downy as those from a pillow.

Where you going in such a hurry? she wheezes.

Upon closer inspection you see they are not feathers at all, but wisps of hair, her scalp spotted with drops of blood.

Name's Renata, she thrusts her freckled fleshy hand toward you. Excuse me! Excuse me!

You step aside to let a girl on a bicycle and a boy on roller skates pass. When you turn back to her, Renata is running after them, her bloodied scarf dangling down her back, feathers of orangey-red hair floating through the air behind her.

She's as loony as a tune, wouldn't you say?

You hadn't seen the young man approaching behind the bicycle child and the roller-skating one. You haven't seen him before at all. He stares at you with blue eyes, like a dog.

You don't got a cigarette, do you?

You shake your head, vigorously. No. Of course not. It goes without saying.

In spite of his stunning white hair, he's no more than five years older than you. He leans closer. I do, he says. Come on.

He doesn't look back. You follow him, stepping aside occasionally for the racing children. You follow him through a labyrinth of halls. After a while he begins to walk slowly, slinking almost. There are no children here, no noise at all. You follow his cue, pressing against the walls. You have an idea you have entered the forbidden area but what are they going to do anyway. Kill you? You snort and he turns those ghost-blue dog eyes on you as though with threat of attack.

You are a body following another body. Your heart is beating against your chest. Hard. Like the fist of a dying man. Let me out, let me out, let me out. You are a body and you are breathing but your breath is not your own.

The body in front of you quickly turns his head, left, right, looking down the long, white hall. The body runs, and your body follows. Because he has your breath now.

What is love? The Doctors ponder this question in various meetings throughout the week. We have been discussing this for years, one of them points out, and still have come to no conclusion. The Doctors agree. There is no formula. No chemical examination. No certainty.

There's been a breech, the Doctor in charge of such matters reports.

The Doctors smile. Let me guess, one of them says, Farino?

But the others don't wait for a confirmation. They know it's Farino.

Who's he with?

They are surprised that it is you. Several of them say this.

The Doctors have a big debate. It lasts for several hours, but in the end, the pragmatists win out. They will not interfere. They must let things run their course. They end with the same question they began with. What is love?

It's quick as the strike of a match to flame. One minute you are a dying body, alone in all the world, and the next you are crouched in a small, windowless room beside a boy whose blue eyes make you tremble, whose breathing, somehow, involves your own. Of course it isn't love. How could it be, so soon? But the possibility exists. He passes the cigarette to you and you hesitate but he says, Whatsa matter? Afraid you're going to get cancer? You place the cigarette between your lips, you draw breath. You do that. He watches you, his blue eyes clouded with smoke.

Thanks. You hand the cigarette back. He flicks the ash onto the floor. The floor is covered with ash. From wall to wall there is ash.

This isn't all mine, you know.

You nod. You don't want to look stupid so you nod. He hands the cigarette to you and your fingers touch momentarily. You are surprised by the thrill this sends through your body. I sing the body electric.

What's that?

You hadn't realized you'd spoken out loud. I sing the body electric, you say. It's from a poem.

You a fucking poet? he says.

You hand the cigarette back to him. Any moment now the Doctors could come and take you away. Any breath could be the last breath. His blue eyes remain locked on yours.

I mean, are you? A fucking poet? He doesn't look away, and you don't either.

You nod.

He grins. He crushes the precious cigarette into the ashy floor. He leans over and his lips meet your lips. He tastes like ash and smoke. The gray powder floats up in the tumble of tossed clothes and writhing bodies. The bodies are coated with a faint gray film and maybe this isn't love, maybe it's only desire, loneliness, infatuation, maybe it's just the body's need, maybe it isn't even happening, maybe you have already been cremated and you are bits of ash creating this strange dream but maybe you are really here, flesh to flesh, ash to ash, alive, breathing, in the possibility of love.

Later, you lie alone on the clean, white sheets in your room. You are waiting. Either he will come for you or they will. You stare at the ceiling. It is dimpled plaster dotted with specks of gold. You think it is beautiful.

Suddenly there is knocking on the door.

You open it but it isn't the Doctors or the police and it isn't him, it's Renata.

Are you naked or dead? she says.

You slam the door. Your ash print remains on the bed, a silhouette of your body, or *the* body. She is knocking and knocking. You tell her to go away but she won't. Exasperated, you grab your ash pants from the floor, step into them, zip and button the fly, open the door.

She is almost entirely bald now, but she still wears that ridiculous paper crown. She sees you looking at it. She reaches up to fondle the point. One of the children made it for me. Behind her you see the evidence of your indiscretion. Your ash footprints reveal your exact course. The hallway is eerily empty.

Where are the children now?

They're gone, she croaks, stepping into the room, a few orange hairs wisping around her. Haven't you noticed how quiet it is?

It is. It is very quiet. All you can hear is her breath, which is surprisingly loud. This place . . . you say, but you don't continue. You were going to say it gives you the creeps but then you remember Farino. Where is he now? How can you hate this place when this is where you found him? You may as well relax. Enjoy this while you can. Soon you will be out there again. Just another dying body without any more chances left.

She opens your closet and begins searching through it. Have you seen my kimono? The one I was wearing when I arrived?

You tell her no. She steps out of the closet, shuts the door. They say it's just like changing clothes, you know.

You nod. You've heard that as well, though you have your doubts.

She sighs. If you see it, will you let me know? She doesn't wait for your reply. She just walks out the door.

You count to ten and then you look down the hall. There is only one set of ash footprints, your own. Are you there? you whisper. Are you there? Are you? Is anyone?

You cannot control the panic. It rises through your body on its own accord. Your throat tightens and suddenly it's as though you are breathing through a straw. Your heart beats wildly against your chest, Let me out, let me out. The body is screaming now. Anyone? Anyone? Is anyone here? But the hall remains empty except for your footprints, the silent ashy steps of your life, and this is when you realize you have not loved enough, you have not breathed enough, you have not even hated enough, and just when you think, well, now it's over, the Doctors come for you, dressed in white smocks spotted with roses of blood and you are pleading with them not to send you back out there with this hopeless body and they murmur hush, hush, and don't worry. But, though they say the right things the words are cold.

They take you down the long, white halls, following your footprints, which, you can only hope (is it possible?) they have not noticed, until, eventually, you pass the room your footprints come out of, smudged into a Rorschach of ash as though several people have walked over them.

Hush, hush. Don't worry. It won't hurt any more than life. That's a little joke. Okay, we're turning here. Yes, that's right. That door. Could you open it, please? No, no, don't back out now. The instruments are sharp but you will be asleep. When you wake up the worst will be over. Here, just lie down. How's that? Okay, now hold still. Don't let the straps alarm you. The body, you know, has its own will to survive. Is that too tight? It is? We don't want it too loose. Once, this was a long time ago, before we perfected the procedure, a body got up right in the middle of it. The body has a tremendous will to survive even when it goes against all reason. What's that? Let's just say it was a big mess and leave it at that. The cigarette? Yes, we know about that. Don't mind the noise, all right? We're just shaving your head. What? Why aren't we angry? Can you just turn this way a little bit? Not really much left here to shave is there? We're not angry; you did your assignment. What's that? Oh, Farino. Of course we know about him. He's right there, didn't you notice? Oh, hey, hey, stop it. Don't be like that. He's fine. He just got here first. He's knocked out already. That's what we're going to do for you now. This might—look, you knew what you were getting into. You already agreed. What do you want? Life or death? You want Farino? Okay, then relax. You've got him.

You are on a train. Your whole body aches. The body is a wound. You groan as you turn your head away from the hard glass. The body is in agony. Your head throbs. You reach up and feel the bald scalp. Oh! The body! The dream of the body! The hope of the body for some miracle world where you will no longer suffer. You press your open palms against your face. You are not weeping. You are not breathing. You are not even here. Someone taps the body's shoulder.

You look up into the hound face of the train conductor. Ticket? he says.

I already gave it to you.

He shakes his head.

You search through your pockets and find a wallet. The wallet is filled with bills but there is no ticket. I seem to have lost it, you say, but look, here, I can pay you.

The conductor lifts the large walkie-talkie to his long mouth and says some words you don't listen to. Then he just stands there, looking at you. You realize he thinks he exists and you do too. The train screams to a long, slow stop. He escorts you off.

You can't just leave me here, you say. I'm not well.

Here's your ride now, he says.

The police cruiser comes to a halt. The policeman gets out. He tilts the brim of his hat at the conductor. When he gets close to you, he looks up with interest, Well, well, he says.

There's been some sort of mistake, you say. Please, I'm not well.

The conductor steps back onto the train. The windows are filled with the faces of passengers. A child with enormous ears points at you and waves. For a second you think you see Farino. But that isn't possible. Is it?

The policeman says, Put your hands behind your back.

These aren't my hands.

He slaps the cuffs on you. Too tight. You tell him they are too tight.

The whistle screams over your words. The train slowly moves away.

Aren't you going to read me my rights?

The policeman leans into your face with bratwurst breath. Just 'cause you shaved your head you think I don't know who you are, he says. He steers you to the cruiser. Places one hand on your head as you crouch to sit in the backseat.

I know my rights, you insist.

He radios the station. Hey, he says, I'm bringing something special.

You drive past cows and cornfields, farmhouses and old barns. The handcuffs burn into your wrists. The head hurts, the arms hurt, the whole body hurts. You groan.

Whatsa matter? The policeman looks at you in the rearview mirror.

I'm not well.

You sure do look beat up.

I've been in a hospital, you say.

Is that right?

You look out the window at an old, white farmhouse on a distant hill. You wonder who loves there.

The station is a little brick building surrounded by scrubby brown grass and pastures. The policeman behind the desk and the policewoman pouring coffee both come over to look at you.

Fucken A, they say.

Can I make my phone call?

The policewoman takes off the handcuffs. She presses the thumb into a pad of ink. She tells you where to stand for your picture. Smile, she says, we got you now Farino.

What?

What is this body doing with you? What has happened? They list the crimes he's committed. You insist it was never you. You never did those things. You are incapable of it. You tell them about the hospital, the Doctors, you tell them how Farino tricked you.

They tell you terrible things. They talk about fingerprints and blood.

But it wasn't me, you insist.

Farino, they say, cut this shit and confess. Maybe we can give you a deal, life, instead of death. How about that?

But I didn't, you say. I'm not like that.

You fucking monster! Why don't you show a little decency? Tell us what you did with the bodies.

I was in a hospital. He switched bodies with me. He tricked me.

Oh fuck it. He's going for the fuckin' insanity shit, ain't he? Fuck it all anyway. How long he been here? Oh, fuck, give him the fuckin phone call. Let him call his fuckin lawyer, the fuckin bastard.

You don't know who to call. They give you the public defender's number. No, you say, I have money. In my wallet.

That ain't your money to spend, you worthless piece of shit. That belonged to Renata King, okay?

Renata?

What? Is it coming back to you now? Your little amnesia starting to clear up?

How'd I end up with Renata's wallet?

You fuckin ape. You know what you did.

But you don't. You only know that you want to live. You want to live more than you want anything else at all. You want life, you want life, you want life. All you want is life.

What if this is really happening? What if you are really here? What if out of all the bodies, all the possibilities, you are in this body and what if it has done terrible things?

Listen, you say. You look up at the three stern faces. They hate you, you think, but no, they hate this body. You are not this body. The stern faces turn away from you. What can you say anyway? How can you explain? You sit, waiting, as though this were an ordinary matter, this beautiful thing, this body, breathing. This body. This past. This terrible judgment. This wonderful knowledge. The body breathes. It breathes and it doesn't matter what you want, when the body wants to, it breathes. It breathes in the hospital, it breathes in the jail, it breathes in your dreams and it breathes in your night-mares, it breathes in love and it breathes in hate and there's not much you can do about any of it, you are on a train, you are in an operating room, you are in a jail, you are innocent, you are guilty, you are not even here. None of this is about you, and it never was.

War Is Beautiful

(Veteran's Day)

WHEN PEOPLE TALK ABOUT VIETNAM, OR MAKE movies about it, all they show you is the blood and sadness there, the dying angels or dark clouds of their souls sinking into the earth like bombs or rising into the sky like smoke, but it was a beautiful place, as strange as a dream. In the morning the valley filled with thick, white fog that no helicopter could get through, we just sat there and watched the fog spire at the top, little wisps that disappeared into a sky which, later, was so blue it looked like it was painted by some kindergartner; the white sand, the fluorescent green rice paddies, the glossy dripping green of the jungle. Sometimes the sky was green. After a while we learned that green sky meant a storm was approaching, black meant there would be monsoon rains that turned the earth to bloody mud. The rain stopped suddenly, as though waved away by God and that blue sky would return, brilliant light brightened the green and gold palms that glowed like wings of angels in the surrounding trees.

The Vietnamese had the prettiest little villages with houses on stilts and wooden steps, which they pulled in at night because of the snakes, which is also why they kept chickens, pigs, geese, and ducks, but especially those chickens that lived under their houses. This was the alarm system they developed, that's how much noise a chicken will make against a snake. These were clever people. They fashioned guns out of old pipes or bits of fence post. They hollowed out part of the trunk of the water palm to catch the clear water that flowed from the palm leaves there. This all seemed so strange to me but it didn't take long before I saw the beauty in it and those Vietnamese girls carrying water, pounding rice, washing clothes in the pond near the pretty little bridge, useless even for such small people, a bridge for the angels, or the spirits who fear water, and these women didn't know we watched them bathe and their children laughing and talking in those strange, loud voices but so beautiful too, with those small, perfect bodies and the dog swimming beside them while the children made toys out of clay; chickens, pigs, and white Brahman cows (such slow, strange creatures), water buffalo that grazed in the fields, slow oxen pulling wagons with large wheels that always seemed a little rickety and sometimes, at night, I can still hear the sound of those wheels turning slowly over the dead.

The war was funny. Nobody talks about that either but it was and how could it not be, humans are funny creatures aren't they, and what is war if not the ultimate in human expression?

In fact, here's a souvenir, a funny pamphlet we dropped, bringing good old American humor to the humorless Vietnamese. "Artillery from our ships will soon hit your village. You must look for cover immediately. From now on, chase the Vietcong away from your village so the government won't have to shell your area again."

Where was God? He had to be laughing, right? He had to see the humor in the super-tall, super-strong, super-weaponed Americans chasing these little men and women in black pajamas in the rain.

Against their pipe-guns we had five or six ammo pouches to a pistol belt, a pair of crossed bandoliers hanging off the chest, a few more on the shoulder, boxed rounds in the pack, spare belts for M60, canteens, a knife, grenades, CS gas and smoke, flak jacket, LBE, M16, All-purpose Lightweight Individual Carrying Equipment pack (otherwise known as Alice), with its heavy metal frame, Claymore mines, more grenades, trip flares, radio batteries, spare ammo for the machine gun, water, C-rations, heat tabs, rope, pull cord (for booby trapped bodies), socks, rifle cleaning kit, bug juice, poncho, cigarettes, extra field dressings, toilet articles, entrenching tool, machete, and can opener.

"Okay soldier. Sling on your LBE. Heave Alice on your back.

Fuck! Port your M16 you stupid fucker, you just going to leave it there for the enemy?"

"Sorry sir."

"Sorry? You're sorry? Dumb shit, you ain't got sorry out here. Sorry is for your little ass in Palooka or wherever the fuck you are from. You're in Vietnam now."

As though we could forget. From the very first day it became obvious that this wasn't a reality any of us had known before.

My angel flutters restless wings beside me and I realize I have gotten off track, what was I talking about? Oh, that's right, how beautiful it all was. I sit here in the fading afternoon sun with my box of souvenirs and remember her, with her beautiful healthy body unbent before me, arms raised, breasts raised, the dark aureole of her raised nipples and the curve of waist to legs all without scars, and I tasted her like holy life, oh life with its beauty and brutality. It's strange, as angels are strange, as God is strange, as we are strange that in this place I should fall in love, falling into her secret dark- ness, the heady scent, the taste of her, a buttock in each hand I raise her up, and I can't get enough, gently I tell her this without words and her small hands on my wrists, her tiny fingers tightening and I am falling into her darkness, her light, her small sounds like cries, like happiness until she arches back, she gasps and I rise up to see her in her glory, all her beauty blossomed, slowly she opens her eyes and this is darkness and this is light and this is forgiveness and this is vengeance and this is our bodies joined like the strange beasts we are exploding with life, blood, limb and flesh joined, alive.

I say, "Binh, I love you" and she laughs. "Why are you laugh- ing?"

She says, "No you say."

"Why, Binh, why?"

She just looks at me with those dark eyes.

I say, "I don't care what you've been, you're my angel now."

"What angel?"

"You know, wings." I spread my arms out wide but she only looks horrified so I point to the ceiling, but she has lived for a long time in a place where only bad things come from the sky. At last, I lie down beside her; hold her in my arms and say, "Beautiful." (That word she knew and she smiled.)

There was no way to tell who or where the enemy was. They could booby trap everything, a cigarette package or soda, we learned early to hold the Coke bottles up to the light to check for broken glass. These were inventive people, they booby trapped the bar girls, women, old people, even children, and after a while it got so it was impossible to tell who the enemy was. We could patrol an area for weeks and continue to lose men, and the people in the village, who pretended not to know anything about these booby traps walked the same trail, "the same fucking trail" as Lenny used to say, day after day and not get hurt, or somebody hits a mine and there's a couple of dead soldiers, and some little rice farmer out in the field doesn't even stop or look up, he's just there picking rice, so after a while it becomes really obvious that these people know where the mines are.

Binh says she can't introduce me to her family because they were killed by U.S. soldiers who came to her village looking to root out communism. The thinking was that if no communists were found then the villagers were hiding them, sort of like the old trick from the witch-burning days when they tied the accused to rocks and dumped them into the lake, the guilty would rise with Satan's magic, the innocent drowned. The villagers crowded into their little hooches and tried to appear friendly, they had seen their own innocent gunned down for running, they'd seen them gunned down for standing still. (The suspicious rice farmer, for instance.) Binh herself, greeted the soldiers while her mother, father, grandmother, little brothers and sisters, and her young son ("You had a son, Binh?") squatted behind her, hopeful expressions on their round faces, for they were a family with someone who spoke English. Binh stood and greeted the soldiers, welcomed them into her home. They laughed, turned, and one of them tossed the grenade, killing all but Binh. There were no communists when the Americans came, said Binh, but there were several when they left. Many, many times, Binh said, America made communists.

Her skin was a miracle, not a single stitch or burn or scar, she was a beautiful girl, a miracle, she said no, not miracle, ghost.

Just because I prefer the company of angels doesn't mean I don't believe in ghosts and there were plenty of them in the jungles of Vietnam, the dark souls of men, women, and children who died in fear, anger, and despair, souls trapped in a jungle that held them there. In the morning you could see them, hovering like green fog everywhere.

Binh said she was a ghost and for a few seconds I saw it, the stretch of skin over bony skeleton, the cavernous dark in her eyes, the way she watched me at times, but I loved her, so I decided no, not ghost, my angel, trapped in this hell. "I will never leave you," I say.

"HA!" she barks the sound, rather loud from someone so small but she watches me closely, not like someone who doesn't care but someone who cares about everything, every little thing I do, like an animal, no, my angel, my lying, desperate girl, my snake.

(There are one hundred thirty-three species of snakes in the jungles of Vietnam and one hundred thirty-one of them are poisonous, if a krait bit you when you first started reading this, you would be dead by now.)

The first guy who spoke to me, I mean really spoke to me was Lenny who just one day starts talking when I was trying to make my dinner, he started talking and I didn't even realize he was talking to me until all of a sudden I did.

"How to cook C-rations is you peel off a piece of C-4, this looks like Turkish Taffy but don't be a dumb shit about it, Pops, okay? You put it in an empty C-ration can, upside down. You gotta have holes in it, see."

"I don't know, cooking with high explosives? What's wrong with just using the heat tabs?"

"Fuck! What'd I care what you use? Do what you want. But if you want your food hot and you're tired of those fumes making your eyes water like I see they are doing then do this. But fuck, don't cook so much you run out of explosives, okay, dumb shit?"

"Thank you, uhm, Lenny, thank you very much, you have no idea how much I — "

Lenny looks at me, squinting like he can't see right, he just stares at me, hard. He had these bright gray-green eyes and a long moustache that draped around his mouth to his chin. "What the fuck am I suppose to do? Let you die? Fuck. You're going to survive this shittin' fuckin' pig sucking hellhole but you ain't been here long enough to thank me yet. Wait until I leave in six months." He pointed to his helmet where he had the months written down and crossed off as they passed. "Let's see if you're thanking me then. Could be you'll hate me by then."

Though I was older than Lenny by many years, I felt like a younger brother. I admired his lean muscles and square hands, his strong legs, the tan defined chest with its swatch of golden hair. When he took a piss and I glanced at his penis in his fist I admired its size and the ease with which his urine flowed, never inhibited, as I was, by others eyes.

But my angel sighs and I sigh too, here, in my kitchen, the gray November sky whispering outside the window, with my shoebox of buttons, pamphlets, squashed cigarettes, the tiny Buddha, a small piece of red tissue paper, and the flower petals, so old that they break apart in my fingers.

The next time I saw Binh, after Lenny died and the terrible things just kept happening, she was already disappearing. I had to squint in the bright room to distinguish her from the light, while my angel was only a dark spot in the corner. She handed me a tiny gift, wrapped in red paper. Even as I opened it I could see that she was fading away, returning to the dead from which everyone came or went including Lenny who saved my life but not his own, and I didn't try to explain this ever before so forgive me please the explosion of words, the ink melted by my tears. I unwrapped it and found a small, gold statue of a man sitting with crossed legs smiling at me, the sweet smile of a fool dressed in a diaper, and it was so strange to see that small smile which held the truth of how funny it all was. I looked up at Binh and she said, "Buddha." I nodded and looked at the little man in my hand and cried while she held me, though of course I was too much for her, all bones and arms and legs and she, so tiny, but she tried to hold me. I curled into a ball with that little gold Buddha in my fist. She didn't say anything at all, just patted my back and my head while I cried.

When I found Lenny he was clutching his gut and he looked up at me with eyes like fire and said, "Oh shit." He kept saying that over and over again as I told him he was going to be all right, but I think we both knew it was a lie. I'm still not sure if he was cursing his wound and his death, or if he was cursing me for being the one to rescue him when the only thing that had kept me alive all that time had been dumb luck and Lenny who I loved, oh man, I loved him and tried to be gentle as I slung him over my back and told him to hang on, his arms wrapped loosely around my neck. Even then he stayed loyal and the best friend I ever knew because I started to fall apart, not arms and legs and guts spilling out falling apart, but inside my soul and everything I was suddenly gone and that's when Lenny starts whispering in my ear, at first I thought it was my angel but it was Lenny and what he's telling me with his last words is to stay calm, to look ahead, to run, and he died on my back and my angel was only a black spot in the distance, absolutely useless and after that it was as though Lenny's spirit had entered me and when the guys found me I was shouting, "Shittin' fuckin' pig suckin, shit rollin' fuckers!"

The last time I saw Binh she was walking down the street with a small boy and an old woman. She didn't even see me. I watched them closely and realized that this was her son, and the old woman was her grandmother. My angel rose from the darkness he had been residing in and spread his great golden wings. Binh looked up, first at my angel, and then at me. She stood there, staring at me until her grandmother said something to her. She spoke to the old woman, and they both looked at me. The boy pulled her hand and she walked away with him while the old woman just stared at me as if I were someone evil. Binh, I thought, now a complete ghost with her dead family, haunting the streets. What other explanation could there be? It's the only thing that made sense.

How I missed Lenny who laughed the first time I told him about her, "Oh man," he said, "You gotta keep those chicks in perspective."

"She's had a hard life," I told him, "her whole family was killed."

Lenny spit and cursed and shook his head. "How much money you giving her, anyway? You better be careful," he said.

I stood on that street, staring into the old woman's eyes until Binh pulled her away, only glancing at me when I called her name. I shouted, but she just kept walking, like a ghost. A few weeks later we come upon a pretty girl picking flowers. She looks up, surprised, when she hears us, her little eyes wide, she drops the basket of blossoms, she turns and runs, her loud voice shouting, who knows what she was saying, she runs shouting, white blossoms spiraling away from her and tangled in her legs, and I shot her and she fell to the ground with the flowers, her coolie hat beside her, limbs at odd angles, her white tunic blossoming red.

"Fuck. What you do that for?"

"She was running sir; I thought she was the enemy."

"Fuck. Goddamn fucker. God damn it." She began to moan, it started out a low sound and soft but it got louder as we stood there. "Fuck! Goddamn it shut her up. Shut. Her. Up."

So I did.

Though my vision is blurred, I see it all so clearly, the tiny black lines of her eyelashes, the infinitesimal pores of her skin, the shape of her small hands like flowers, the rising of her chest beneath the growing red, the way her mouth formed a blood blossom. And before everything and after everything there is this strange reckoning, her body bounced, once, twice, the jerk of limbs, a flower spasm, and that moment, that small, unforgettable moment, when she looked at me, what did she see, her black eyes, rolling like tossed marbles, and then finding me, looking right at me, and locked there forever, as though on something beautiful.

The Christmas Witch

(Thanksgiving / Christmas)

*T*HE CHILDREN OF STONE COLLECT BONES, FOL-
lowing cats through twisted, narrow streets, chasing them
away from tiny birds, dead gray mice (with sweet round ears, pink
inside like seashells), and fish washed on rocky shore. The children
show each other their bone collections, tiny white femurs, infinitesimal wings, jawbones with small teeth intact. Occasionally, parents find these things; they scold the little hoarder, or encourage the
practice by setting up a science table. It's a stage children go
through, they assume, this fascination with structure, this cold
approach to death. The parents do not discuss it with each other,
except in passing. ("Oh yes, the skeleton stage.") The parents do not
know, they do not guess that once the found bones are tossed out or
put on display, the children begin to collect again. They collect in
earnest.

Rachel Boyle has begun collecting bones, though her father
doesn't know about it, of course. Her mother, being dead, might
know. Rachel can't figure that part out. Her mother is not a ghost,
the Grandma told her, but a spirit. The Grandma lives far away, in
Milwaukee. Rachel didn't even remember her when she came for
the funeral. "You remember me, honey, don't you?" she asked and
Rachel's father said, "Of course she remembers you." Rachel went

in the backyard where she tore flowers while her father and the Grandma sat at the kitchen table and cried. After the Grandma left, Rachel and her father moved to Stone.

Rachel doesn't get off the school bus at her house, because her father is still at work. She gets off at Peter Williamson's house. The first time she found Peter with his bone collection spread out before him on the bedroom floor she thought it was gross. But the second time she sat across from him and asked him what they were for.

Peter shrugged. "You know," he said.

Rachel shook her head.

"Didn't they teach you anything in Boston? They're for Wilmot Redd, the witch. You know. A long time ago. An old lady. She lived right here in Stone. They hung her. There's a sign about her on Old Burial Hill but she's not buried there. No one knows where she ended up."

That's when Rachel began collecting bones. She stored them in her sock drawer, she stored them under her bed, she had several in her jewelry box, and two chicken legs buried in the flowerpot from her mother's funeral. The flowers were dead, but it didn't matter, she wouldn't let her father throw them out.

For Halloween, Rachel wants to be dead but her father says she can't be. "How about a witch?" he says, "Or a princess?"

"Peter's going to be dead," she says. "He'll have a knife going right through the top of his head, and blood dripping down his face."

"How about a cat? You can have a long tail and whiskers."

"Mariel is going to be a pilgrim."

"You can be a pilgrim."

"Pilgrims are dead! Jeez, Dad, didn't they teach you anything in Boston?"

"Don't talk to me like that."

Rachel sighs, "Okay, I'll be a witch."

"Fine, we'll paint your face green and you can wear a wig."

"Not that kind of witch."

Her father turns out the light and kisses her on the forehead before he leaves her alone in the dark. All of a sudden Rachel is scared. She thinks of calling her father. Instead, she counts to fifty before she pulls back the covers and sneaks around in the dark of her room, gathering the bones, which she pieces together into a sort of puzzle shape of a funny little creature, right on top of her bed. She uses a skull, and a long bone that might be from a fish, the small shape of a mouse paw, and a couple of chicken legs. She sucks her thumb while she waits for it to do the silly dance again.

On Tuesday, Mrs. Williamson has a doctor's appointment. Rachel still gets off the bus with Peter. They still go to his house. There, the baby-sitter waits for them. Her name is Melinda. She has long, blonde hair, a pierced navel, pierced tongue, ears pierced all the way around the edge, and rings on every finger. She wraps her arms around Peter and wrestles him to the floor. He screams but he is smiling. After a while she lets go and turns to Rachel.

Rachel wishes Melinda would wrap her arms around her, but she doesn't. "My name's Melinda," she says. Rachel nods. Her father already told her. He wouldn't let her be watched by a stranger. "Who wants popcorn?" Melinda says and races Peter into the kitchen. Rachel follows even though she doesn't really like popcorn.

Peter tells Melinda about his plans for Halloween. He tells her about the knife through his head while the oil heats up in the pan. Melinda tosses in a kernel. Peter runs out of the room.

"What are you going to be?" Melinda asks but before Rachel can answer, Peter is back in the kitchen, the knife in his head, blood dripping around the eyes. Melinda says, "Oh gross, that's so great, it looks really gross." The kernel pops. Melinda pours more kernels into the pan and then slaps the lid on. "Hey, dead man," she says, "How about getting the butter?"

Peter gets a stick of butter out of the refrigerator. He places it on the cutting board. He takes a sharp knife out of the silverware drawer. Popcorn steam fills the kitchen. Rachel feels sleepy, sitting at the island. She leans her head into her hand; her eyes droop. Peter makes a weird sound and drops the knife on the counter. Blood trickles from his finger and over the butter. Melinda sets the pan on a cold burner, turns off the stove, and wraps Peter's finger in a paper towel. Rachel isn't positive but she thinks Peter is crying beneath his mask.

"It's okay," Melinda says. "It's just a little cut." She steers Peter through the kitchen toward the bathroom. Rachel looks at the blood on the butter; one long, red drop drips down the side. She stares at the kitchen window, foggy with steam. For a second she thinks someone is standing out there, watching, but no one is. Peter and Melinda come back into the kitchen. Peter no longer has the knife through his head. His hair is stuck up funny, his face, pink, and he has a Band-Aid on his finger. He sits at the island beside Rachel but doesn't look at her. Melinda slices the bloody end of butter and tosses it into the trash. She cuts a chunk off, places it in a glass bowl and sticks it in the microwave. "So, what are you going to be for Halloween?"

"Wilmot Redd," Rachel says.

"You can't," says Melinda.

"Don't you know anything?" Peter asks.

"Be nice, Peter." Melinda pours the popcorn into a big, purple bowl and drips melted butter over it. "You can't be Wilmot Redd."

"Why not?"

Melinda puts ice in three glasses and fills them with Dr. Pepper. She sits down at the island, across from Peter and Rachel. "If I tell you, you can't tell your dad."

Rachel has heard about secrets like this. When a grownup tells you not to tell your parents something, it is a bad secret. Rachel is thrilled to be told one. "I won't," she says.

"Okay, I know you think witches wear pointy black hats and act like the bad witch in *The Wizard of Oz* but they don't. Witches are just regular people and they look and dress like everyone else. Stone is full of witches. I can't tell you who all is a witch, but you would be surprised. Who knows? Maybe you'll grow up to be a witch yourself. All that stuff about witches is a lie. People have been lying about witches for a very long time. And that's what happened to Wilmot Redd. Maybe she wasn't even a witch at all, but one thing for sure she wasn't an evil witch. That's the part that's made up about witches and that's what they made up about her, and that's how come she wound up dead. You can't dress up as Wilmot Redd. We just don't make fun of her in Stone. Even though it happened a long time ago, most people here still feel really bad about it. Most people think she was just an old woman who was into herbs and shit, don't tell your dad I said 'shit' either, all right? Making fun of Wilmot Redd is like saying you think witches should be hung. You don't think that do you? All right then, so don't dress up as Wilmot Redd. You can go as a made-up witch, but leave poor Wilmot Redd out of it. No one even knows what happened to her, I mean after she died. That's how much she didn't matter. They threw her body off a cliff somewhere. No one even knows where her bones ended up. They could be anywhere."

"Do you collect bones?" Rachel asks and Peter kicks her.

"Why would I do that?" Melinda says. "You have some weird ideas, kid."

*   *   *

Witches everywhere. Teacher witches, mommy and daddy witches, policeman witches too, boy witches and girl witches, smiling witches, laughing witches, bus driver witches. Who is not a witch in Stone? Rachel isn't, she knows that for sure.

Rachel makes special requests for chicken "with the bones," she says, and she eats too much, giving herself a stomachache.

"How many bones do you need?" her father asks, because Rachel has told him she needs them for a school project.

"I don't know," she says. "Jack just keeps saying I need more."

"Jack sounds kind of bossy," her father says.

Rachel nods. "Yeah, but he's funny too."

Finally, Halloween arrives. Rachel goes to school dressed as a made-up witch. She notices that there are several of them on the bus and the playground. They start the morning with doughnuts and apple cider and then they do math with questions like two pumpkins plus one pumpkin equals how many pumpkins.

Rachel raises her hand and the lady at the front of the room who says she is Miss Engstrom, their teacher, but who doesn't look anything like her, says, "Yes, Rachel?"

"How many bones does it take to make a body?"

"That's a very good question," the lady says. She's wearing a long, purple robe and she has black hair that keeps sliding around funny on her head. "I'll look that up for you, Rachel, but in the meantime, can you answer my question? You have two pumpkins and then your mother goes to the store and comes home with one more pumpkin, how many pumpkins do you have?"

"Her mother is dead," a skeleton in the back of the room says.

"I don't care," says Rachel.

"I mean your father," the lady says. "I meant to say your father goes to the store."

But Rachel just sits there and the lady calls on someone else.

They get an extra long recess. Cindi Becker tears her princess dress on the swing and cries way louder than Peter cried when he cut his finger. Somebody dressed all in black, with a black hood, won't speak to anyone but walks slowly through the playground, stopping occasionally to point a black-gloved finger at one of the children. When one of the kindergartners gets pointed at, he runs, screaming, back to his teacher, who is dressed up as a pirate.

Rachel finds Peter with the knife in his head and says, "Don't tell, but I'm still going to be Wilmot Redd tonight." The boy turns to her, but doesn't say anything at all, just walks away. After a while, Rachel realizes that there are three boys on the playground with knives in their heads, and she isn't sure if the one she spoke to was Peter.

They don't have the party until late in the afternoon. The lady who says she is Miss Engstrom turns off the lights and closes the drapes.

Rachel raises her hand. The lady nods at her.

"When my mom went to the store a bad man shot her—"

The lady waves her arms, as if trying to put out a fire, the purple sleeves dangling from her wrists. "Rachel, Rachel," she says. "I'm so sorry about your mother. I should have said your father went to the store. I'm really sorry. Maybe I should tell a story about witches."

"My mother is not a witch," Rachel says.

"No, no of course she's not a witch. Let's play charades!"

Rachel sits at her desk. She is a good girl for the most part. But she has learned that even without her face painted, she can pretend to be listening when she isn't. Nobody notices that she isn't playing their stupid game. Later, when she is going to the bus, the figure all dressed in black points at her. She feels the way the kindergartner must have felt. She feels like crying. But she doesn't cry.

She gets off the bus at Peter Williamson's house with Peter who acts crazy, screaming for no reason, letting the door slam right in her face. *I hate you, Peter,* she thinks, and is surprised to discover that nothing bad happens to her for having this thought. But when she opens the door, Melinda is standing there, next to Peter who still has the knife in his head. "Don't you understand? You can't dress up as Wilmot Redd."

"Where's Mrs. Williamson?" Rachel asks.

"She had to go to the doctor's. Did you hear me?"

"I'm not," Rachel says, walking past Melinda. "Can't you see I'm just a made-up witch?"

"Is that what you're wearing tonight?"

Rachel nods.

"Who wants popcorn?" Melinda says. Rachel sticks her tongue out at Peter. He just stands there, with the knife in his head.

"Hey, aren't you guys hungry?" Melinda calls from the kitchen.

Peter runs, screaming, past Rachel. She walks in the other direction, to Peter's room. She knows where he keeps his collection, in his bottom drawer. Peter hasn't said anything about it, maybe he hasn't noticed, but Rachel has been stealing bones from him for some time now. Today she takes a handful. She doesn't have any pockets so she drops the bones into her Halloween treat bag from school. She is careful not to set the bag down. She is still carrying it when her father comes to get her.

They walk home together, through the crooked streets of Stone. The sky is turning gray. Ghosts and witches dangle from porches and crooked trees behind picket fences. Pumpkins grin blackly at her.

Rachel's father says that after dinner Melinda is coming over.

"She just wants to see what kind of witch I am," Rachel says.

Her father smiles, "Yes, I'm sure you're right. Also, I asked her if she could stay and pass out treats while I go with you. That way no one will play a trick on us."

"Melinda might," Rachel says, but her father just laughs, as if she were being funny.

When they get home, Rachel goes into her bedroom while her father makes dinner. He's making macaroni and cheese, her favorite, though tonight the thought of it makes her strangely queasy. Rachel begins to gather the bones from all the various hiding places, the box under her bed, the sock drawer. She puts them in a pillowcase. When her father calls her for dinner, she shoves the pillowcase under her bed.

In the kitchen, a man stands next to the stove with a knife in his head. Rachel screams, and her father tears off the mask. He tells her he's sorry. "See," he lifts the mask up by the knife. "It's just something I bought at the drugstore. I thought it would be funny."

Rachel tries to eat but she doesn't have much of an appetite. She picks at the yellow noodles until the doorbell rings. Her father answers it and comes back with Melinda who smiles and says, "How's the little witch?"

"Not dead," Rachel answers.

Rachel's father looks at her as if she has a knife in her head.

They go from house to house begging for candy. The witches of Stone drop M&M's, peanut butter cups, and popcorn balls into Rachel's plastic pumpkin. Once, a ghost answers the door, and once, when she reaches into a bowl for a small Hershey's bar, a green hand pops up through the candy and tries to grab her. Little monsters, giant spiders, made-up witches, and bats weave gaily around Rachel and her father. The pumpkins, lit from within, grin at her. Rachel thinks of Wilmot Redd standing on Old Burial

Hill watching all of them, waiting for her to bring the bones.

But when Rachel gets home, the bones are gone. The pillow-case, filled with most of her collection and shoved under her bed, is missing. Rachel runs into the living room, just in time to see Melinda leaving with a white bundle under her arm. Rachel stands there, in her fake witch costume and thinks, *I wish you were dead.* She has a lot of trouble getting to sleep that night. She cries and cries and her father asks her over and over again if it's because of her mother. Rachel doesn't tell him about the bones. She doesn't know why. She just doesn't.

Two days later, Melinda is killed in a car accident. Rachel's father wipes tears from his eyes when he tells her. Mrs. Williamson cries when she thinks Peter and Rachel aren't watching. But Peter and Rachel don't cry.

"She stole my bones," Rachel says.

"Mine too," says Peter. "She stole a bunch of them."

Melinda's school picture is on the front page of the newspaper, beside a photograph of the fiery wreck.

"That's what she gets," Rachel says, "for stealing."

Peter frowns at Rachel.

"Wanna trade?" she asks.

He nods. Rachel trades a marshmallow pumpkin for a small bone shaped like a toe.

That night, after her father kisses her on the forehead and turns off the light, she takes her small collection of bones and tries to make them dance, but the shape is all wrong. It just lies there and doesn't do anything at all.

The day of Melinda's funeral, Rachel's father doesn't go to work. He's a lawyer in Boston and it isn't easy, the way it is for some par-ents, to stay home on a workday, but he does. He picks Rachel up at school just after lunch.

The funeral is in a church in the new section of Stone, far from the harbor and Old Burial Hill. On the way there, they pass a group of people carrying signs.

"Close your eyes," her father says.

Rachel closes her eyes. "What are they doing?"

"They're protesting. They're against abortion."

"What's abortion?"

"Okay, you can open them. Abortion is when a woman is preg-nant and decides she doesn't want to be pregnant."

"You mean like magic?"

"No, it's not magic. She has a procedure. The procedure is

called having an abortion. When that's over, she's not pregnant any-more."

Rachel looks out the car window at the pumpkins with collapsed faces, the falling ghosts, a giant spiderweb dangling in a tree. "Dad?" "Mmhm?"

"Can we move back to Boston?"

Her father glances down at her. "Don't you feel safer here? And you already have so many friends. Mrs. Williamson says you and Peter get along great. And there's your friend, Jack. Maybe we can have him over some Saturday."

"Melinda said there are a lot of witches in Stone."

Her father whistles, one long low sound. "Well, she was probably just trying to be funny. Here we are." They are parked next to a church. "This is where Melinda's funeral is."

"Okay," says Rachel but neither of them move to get out of the car.

"Let's say a prayer for Melinda," her father says.

"Here?"

He closes his eyes and bows his head while Rachel watches a group of teenage girls in cheerleading uniforms hugging on the church steps.

"Now, do you wanna get ice cream?"

Rachel can't believe she's heard right. She knows about funerals and they don't have anything to do with ice cream, but she nods, and he turns the car around, right in the middle of the street, just as the church bells ring. Rachel's father drives all the way back to the old section of Stone, where they stop for ice cream. Rachel has pep-permint stick and her father has vanilla. They walk on the sidewalk next to the water and watch the seagulls. Rachel tries not to think about Wilmot Redd who stands on Old Burial Hill, waiting.

Her father looks at his watch. "We have to get going," he says. "It's almost time for Peter to get off the bus."

"Peter?"

"His mother has to go to the doctor's. I told her he could come to our house."

Rachel's father goes out to meet Peter when he gets off the bus and they walk in together, talking about the Red Sox. They walk right past Rachel. "Dad?" she says but he doesn't answer. She fol-lows them into the kitchen. Her father is spreading cream cheese on a bagel for Peter. Later, when she is playing in her bedroom with him, Rachel says, "I wish your mom had an abortion," which makes Peter cry. When her father comes into the room he makes her tell him what she did and she tells him she didn't do anything but Peter tells on her and her father says she is grounded.

Miss Engstrom tells them that they are very lucky to live in Stone, so near to Danvers and Salem and the history of witches. Rachel says that she knows there are a lot of witches in Stone and Miss Engstrom laughs and then all the children laugh too. Later, on the playground, Stella Miner and Leanne Green hold hands and stick out their tongues at Rachel, and Minnity Dover throws pebbles at her. Miss Engstrom catches Minnity and makes her sit on the bench for the rest of recess. Rachel swings so high that she can imagine she is flying. When the bell rings, she comes back to Earth where Bret and Steve Keeter, the twins, and Peter Williamson wait for her. "We wish your mom had an abortion," Peter says. The twins nod their golden heads.

"You don't even know what that means," says Rachel and runs past them, toward Miss Engstrom who stands beside the open door, frowning.

"Rachel," she says, "You're late." But she doesn't say anything to the boys, who come in behind Rachel, whispering.

"Shut up!" Rachel shouts.

Miss Engstrom sends Rachel to the office. The principal says he is going to call her father. Rachel sits in the office until it's almost time to go home, and then she goes back to the classroom for her books and lunchbox.

"Wanna know what we did while you were gone?" Clara Vanmeer whispers when they line up for the bus.

Rachel ignores her. She knows what they did. They are witches, all of them, and they put some kind of spell on her. *I wish you were all dead*, Rachel thinks, and she really means it. It worked with Melinda, didn't it? But not her mom. She never wished her mom would die. Never never never. Who did? Who wished that for her mother who used to call her Rae-Rae and made chocolate chip pancakes and was beautiful? Rachel hugs her backpack and stares out the window at the witches of Stone, picking their kids up from school. The bus drives past rotten pumpkins and fallen graveyards. Rachel's head hurts. She hopes Mrs. Williamson will let her take a nap but when they get there, the house is locked. Peter rings the doorbell five hundred times, and pulls on the door but Rachel just sits on the step. Nobody is home, why can't he just get that through his head? Finally, Peter starts to cry. "Shut up," Rachel says. She has to say it twice before he does.

"Where's my mother?" Peter asks, wiping his nose with the sleeve of his jacket.

"How should I know?" Rachel watches a small, black cat with a tiny, silver bell around its neck emerge from the bush at the neighbor's house. Unfortunately, it is not carrying a dead bird or mouse. Peter starts crying again. Loudly. Rachel's head hurts. "Shut up!" she says, but he just keeps crying. She stands up and readjusts her backpack.

Rachel is already walking down the tiny sidewalk when Peter calls for her to wait. They walk to Rachel's house, but of course that is locked as well. Peter starts crying again. Rachel takes off the backpack and sets it on the step. The afternoon sun is low, the sky gray and fuzzy like a sweater. Her head hurts and she's hungry. Also, Peter is really annoying her, "I want my mother," he says.

"Well, I want my mother too," Rachel says. "But that doesn't help. She's dead, okay? She's dead."

"My mom's dead?" Peter screams, so loud that Rachel has to cover her ears with her hands. That's when Mrs. Williamson comes running up the sidewalk. Peter doesn't even see her at first because he's so hysterical. Mrs. Williamson runs to Peter. She sits down beside him, says his name, and touches him on the shoulder. He looks up and shouts, "Mom!" He wraps his arms around her, saying over and over again, "You're not dead." Rachel resists the temptation to look down the sidewalk to see if her own mother is coming. She knows she is not.

They walk back to the Williamsons' house together. Rachel, trying not to drag her backpack, follows. "I'm sorry," she hears Mrs. Williamson say. "I had a doctor's appointment and I got caught in traffic. I tried to call the school, but I was too late, and then I tried to find someone to come to the house, but no one was home."

Peter says something to Mrs. Williamson. She can't hear him and she leans over so he can whisper in her ear. Rachel stands behind them, watching. Mrs. Williamson turns and stares at Rachel. "Did you tell him I was dead?" she asks.

Rachel shakes her head no, but she can tell Mrs. Williamson doesn't believe her.

"When the Pilgrims came to America they wanted to live in a place where they could practice their religion. They were trying to be good people. So when they saw someone doing something they thought was bad, they wanted to stop it. Bad meant the devil to them. They didn't want to be around the devil. They wanted to be around God." Miss Engstrom stands at the front of the room dressed as a Puritan. She puts the Puritan dress on every day for Social Studies. Her cheeks are pink and her hair is sticking to her face. She is trying to help them understand what happened, she says, but Cindi Becker has said, more than once, that her mom doesn't want Miss Engstrom teaching them religion. "It's not religion," Miss Engstrom says, "it's History."

Every day Miss Engstrom puts on the Pilgrim dress and pretends she's a Puritan. The children are supposed to pretend they are witches. "Act natural," she tells them. "Just be yourselves." But when they do, they get in trouble; they have to stand in the stockade or go to the jail in the back of the room. The stockade is made out of cardboard, and the jail is just chairs in a circle. Rachel hates to be put in either place. By the fourth lesson, she has figured out how to sit at her desk with her hands neatly folded. When Miss Engstrom asks Rachel what she is doing, she says, "Praying" and Miss Engstrom tells her what a good Puritan she is. By the sixth lesson the class is filled with good Puritans,. sitting with neatly folded hands. Only Charlie Dexter is stuck in the stockade and Cindi Becker is in the jail in the back of the room. Miss Engstrom says that they are probably witches. Rachel decides that Social Studies is her favorite subject. She looks forward to the next lesson. What will happen to the witches when they go on trial? But the next day they have a substitute and the day after that, another. They have so many substitutes Rachel can't remember their names. One day, one of the substitutes tells the class that she is their new teacher.

"What happened to Miss Engstrom?" Rachel asks.

"My mother had her fired," says Cindi Becker.

"She's not coming back," the teacher says. "Now, let's talk about Thanksgiving."

Rachel is so excited about Thanksgiving she can't stand it. A whole turkey! Think of the bones! Each night Rachel rearranges her bone collection. It is a difficult time of year for it. Cats still wander the crooked streets of Stone but they are either eating everything they kill, or killing less, because there are few bones to be found. Rachel arranges and rearranges, trying to form the shape that will dance for her. Damn that Melinda, Rachel thinks. What would happen if Rachel had bones like that in her collection? Human bones?

Rachel has a fit when her father tells her they are going to the Williamsons' house for Thanksgiving. "This will be better," he says.

"You can play with Peter and his cousins. Don't you think it would be lonely with just you and me at our house?"

"The bones!" Rachel cries. "I want the bones!"

"What are you talking about?" her father asks.

Rachel sniffs. "I want the turkey bones."

Rachel's father stares at her. He is cutting an apple and he stands, holding the knife, staring at her.

"You know, for my project."

"Are you still doing that, now that Miss Engstrom is gone?"

Rachel nods. Her father says, "Well, we can make a turkey. But not on Thursday. On Thursday we're going to the Williamsons'."

The night before Thanksgiving though, her father gets a phone call. He says, "Oh, I am so sorry." And, "No, no please don't even worry about us." He nods his head a lot. "Please know you are in our prayers. Let us know if we can do anything." After he hangs up the phone he sits in his chair and stares at the TV screen. Finally, he says, "It looks like you got your wish."

He looks at his watch, and then, all in a hurry, they drive to the grocery store, where he buys a turkey, bags of stuffing, and pumpkin pie. He throws the food into the cart. Rachel can tell that he is angry but she doesn't ask him what's wrong. She'd rather not know. Besides, she has other stuff to worry about. Like is there a bad man in this store? Will he shoot them the way he shot her mother?

When they get home her father says, "Mrs. Williamson lost the baby."

"What baby?" Rachel asks.

"She was pregnant. But she lost it."

Rachel remembers, once, when Mrs. Williamson got angry at Peter when he came home from school without his sweater. "You can't be so careless all the time," Rachel remembers her saying.

"Well, she shouldn't be so careless," Rachel says.

"Rachel, you have to start learning to think about other people's feelings once in a while."

Rachel thinks about the lost baby, out in the dark somewhere. "Mrs. Williamson is stupid," she says.

Rachel's father, holding a can of cranberry sauce with one hand, points toward her room with the other. "You go to your room," he says. "And think about what you're saying."

Rachel runs to her room. She slams the door shut. She throws herself on her bed and cries herself to sleep. When she wakes up there is no light shining under the door. She doesn't know what time it is, but she thinks it is very late. She gets up and begins collecting bones from all the hiding places; bones in her socks, bones in her underwear drawer, bones in a box under the bed, bones in her jewelry box, and bones in her stuffed animals, cut open with the scissors she's not supposed to use. She hums as she assembles and reassembles the bones until at last they quiver and shake. She thinks they are going to dance for her but instead, they stab her with their sharp little points.

"Stop it," Rachel says. She takes them apart again, stores them in separate places and goes to sleep, crying for her mother.

The next morning, Rachel watches the parade on TV while her father makes stuffing and cleans the turkey. When the phone rings, he brings it to Rachel, and turns the TV sound off. The Grandma asks her how school is going and how she likes living in Stone, and finally, how is she? Rachel answers each question, "Fine," while watching a silent band march across the TV. The Grandma asks to speak to her father again and Rachel goes to the kitchen. Her father reaches for the phone and says, "My God, Rachel, what happened to your arms?" Rachel looks down at her arms. There are small red spots and tiny bruises all over them.

"She has bruises all over her arms," her father says.

Rachel grabs a stick of celery and walks toward the living room. Her father follows, still holding the phone. "Rachel, what happened to your arms?"

Rachel turns and smiles at him. Ever since her mom died, her dad has been trying hard. Rachel knows this, and she knows that he doesn't know she knows this. But there are certain things he isn't very good at. Rachel is positive that if her mom were still alive, she wouldn't even have to ask what had happened, she'd know. Rachel feels sorry for her dad but she doesn't want to tell him about the bones. Look what happened when she barely even mentioned them to Melinda. So Rachel makes something up instead. "Miss Engstrom," she says.

"What are you talking about? Miss Engstrom? She isn't even your teacher anymore."

Rachel only smiles, sweetly, at her father. He repeats what she told him, into the phone. Rachel walks into the living room. She wraps herself in the red throw and sits in front of the TV, watching the balloon man fill up the screen as she munches on celery. How many bones does it take, anyway? Miss Engstrom never did answer her question.

Later, when the doorbell rings, her father shouts, "I'll get it," which is sort of strange because she is never allowed to answer the door. She hears voices and then her father comes into the room with a policeman and a policewoman. Rachel thinks they've come to arrest her. She's a liar, a thief, and a murderer, so it had to happen. Still, she feels like crying now that it has.

Her father has been talking to her, she realizes, but she has no idea what he's said. He turns the sound off the TV and he and the policeman walk out of the room together. The policewoman stays with Rachel. She sits right next to Rachel on the couch. For a while they watch the silent parade, until the policewoman says, "Can you tell me what happened to your arms, Rachel?"

"I already told my dad," Rachel says.

The policewoman nods. "The thing is, I just want to make sure he didn't leave anything out."

"I don't want to get in trouble."

"You're not in trouble. We are here to help. Okay, honey? Can I see your arms?"

Rachel shakes her head, no.

The policewoman nods. "Who hurt you, Rachel?"

Rachel turns to look at her. She has blonde hair and brown eyes with yellow flecks in them. She looks at Rachel very closely. As if she knows the truth about her.

"You can tell me," she says.

"The bones," Rachel whispers.

"What about the bones?"

"But you can't tell anyone."

"I might have to tell someone," the policewoman says.

So Rachel refuses to speak further. She shows the lady her arms, but only because she figures it will make her go away, and it does. After she looks at Rachel's arms the policewoman goes out in the kitchen with her dad and the policeman. Rachel turns up the volume. Jessica Simpson, dressed in white fur, like a kitten without the whiskers, is singing. Her voice fills up the room, but Rachel can still hear the murmuring sound of the grownups talking in the kitchen. Then the door opens and closes and she hears her father saying good-bye. Rachel's father comes and stands in the room, watching her. He doesn't say anything and Rachel doesn't either but later, when they are eating turkey together he says, "You might still be just a little girl but you can get grownups in a lot of trouble by telling lies."

Rachel nods. She knows this. Miss Engstrom taught them all

about the history of witches. Rachel chews the turkey leg clean. It was huge and she is quite full, but now she has a turkey leg, almost as big as a human bone, to add to her collection. She sets it on her napkin next to her plate. As if he can read her mind her father says, "Rachel, no more bones."

"What?"

"Your bone collection. It's done. Over. Find something else to collect. Seashells. Buttons. Barbie dolls. No more bones."

Rachel knows better than to argue. Instead, she asks to be excused. Her father doesn't even look at her; he just nods. Rachel goes to her bedroom and searches through the mess of clothes in the wicker chair until she finds her Halloween costume. When her father comes to tell her it's time for bed, he says, "You can wear that one last time but then we're putting it away until next year."

"Can I sleep in it?" Rachel asks.

Her father shrugs. "Sure, why not?" He smiles, but it is a pretend smile. Rachel smiles a pretend smile back. She crawls into bed, dressed like a pretend witch. Her father kisses her on the forehead and turns out the light. Rachel lies there until she counts to a hundred and then she sits up. She gathers the bones, whispering in the dark.

A few days later, the witch costume has been packed away, the first dusting of snow has sprinkled the crooked streets and picket fences of Stone, and Rachel has forgotten all about how angry she was at her father. Since Mrs. Williamson lost the baby, she no longer watches Rachel. Rachel thinks this is a good idea because she doesn't feel safe with Mrs. Williamson, but she hates being in school all day. All the other children have been picked up from the after school program and it's just Rachel and Miss Carrie who keep looking out the school window, saying, "Boy, your dad sure is late."

Rachel sits at the play table, making a design with the purple, blue, green, and yellow plastic shapes. She is good at putting things together and Miss Carrie compliments her work. Rachel remembers putting the spell on her father and she regrets it. She pretends the shapes are bones, she puts them together and then she takes them apart, she whispers, trying to say the words backward, but it is hard to do and Miss Carrie, who isn't a real grownup at all, but a high school girl like Melinda, says, "Uh, you're starting to creep me out."

Miss Carrie calls her mother, using the purple cell phone she carries in the special cell phone pocket of her jeans. "I don't know what to do," she says. "Rachel is still here. Her dad is really late. Hey, Rache, what's your last name again?" Rachel tells Carrie and Carrie tells her mom. Just then, Mrs. Williamson arrives. She is wearing a raincoat, even though it isn't raining, and her hair is a mess. She tells Carrie that she is taking Rachel home. Rachel doesn't want to go with Mrs. Williamson, the baby loser, but Carrie says, "Oh, great," to Mrs. Williamson and then says into the phone, "Never mind, someone finally came to pick her up." She is still talking to her mother when Rachel leaves with Mrs. Williamson who doesn't say anything until they are in the car.

"Peter told me what you said, Rachel, about how I should have had an abortion, and I want you to know, that sort of talk is not allowed in our house. I really don't even want you playing with Peter anymore. Not one word about abortion or dead mothers or anything else you have up your sleeve, do you understand?"

Rachel nods. She is looking out the window at a house decorated with tiny, white icicle lights hanging over the windows. "Where's my dad?" she asks.

Mrs. Williamson sighs, "He's been delayed."

Rachel is afraid to ask what that means. When they get to the Williamsons' house, Mrs. Williamson pretends to be nice. She asks Rachel if her book bag is too heavy and offers to carry it. Rachel shakes her head. She is afraid to say anything for fear that it will be the wrong thing. There is a big wreath on the back door of the Williamsons' house and it has a bell on it that rings when they go inside. Mr. Williamson and Peter are eating at the kitchen table. The house is deliciously warm but it smells strange.

Mrs. Williamson takes off her raincoat and hangs it from a peg in the wall. Rachel drops her book bag below the coats, and stands there until Mrs. Williamson tells her to hang up her coat and sit at the table.

When Rachel sits down Mr. Williamson points a chicken leg at her and says, "Now listen here, young lady—" but Mrs. Williamson interrupts him.

"I already talked to her," she says.

Rachel is mashing her peas into her potatoes when her father arrives. He thanks Mr. and Mrs. Williamson and he says, "How you doing?" to Peter though Peter doesn't answer. Mrs. Williamson invites him to stay for dinner but he says thank you, he can't. Rachel leaves her plate on the table and no one tells her to clear it. She puts on her coat. Her father picks up her backpack. He thanks the Williamsons again and then taps Rachel's shoulder. Hard.

"Thank you," Rachel says.

They walk out to the car together, their shoes squeaking on the snow. The Williamsons' house is decorated with white lights; the neighbors have colored lights and two big plastic snowmen with frozen grins and strange eyes on their front porch.

"What did you say to that policewoman?" Rachel's father asks.

He isn't looking at Rachel. He is staring out the window, the way he does when he is driving in Boston.

"Miss Engstrom didn't do it," she says.

"They seem to think I hurt you, do you understand—" He doesn't finish what he is saying. He pulls into their driveway, but instead of getting out of the car to open the garage door, he sits there. "Just tell the truth, Rachel, okay? Just tell the truth. You know what that is, don't you?"

"I did," Rachel says. She feels like crying and also, she thinks she might throw up.

"Who did that to you, then? Who did that to your arms?"

"The bones."

"The bones?"

Rachel nods.

"What bones?"

"You know."

Her father makes a strange noise. He is bent over, and his eyes are shut. Praying, Rachel thinks. The car is still running. Rachel looks out the window. She cranes her neck so she can see the Sheekles' yard. They have it decorated with six reindeer made out of white lights. The car door slams. Rachel watches her father open the garage door. She watches him walk back to the car, lit by the headlights, his neck bent as if he is looking for something very important that he has lost.

"Dad?" Rachel says when he gets back in the car. "Are you mad?"

He shakes his head. He eases the car into the garage, turns off the ignition. They walk to the house together. When they get inside, he says, "Okay, I want all of them."

"All of what?" Rachel says, though she thinks she knows.

"That bone collection of yours. I want it."

"No, Dad."

He shakes his head. He stands there in his best winter coat, his gloves still on, shaking his head. "Rachel, why would you want to keep them, if they are hurting you?"

It's a good question. Rachel has to think for a moment before she answers. "Not all the time," she says. "Mostly they don't. They used to be my friend."

"The bones?"

Rachel nods.

"The bones used to be your friend?"

"Jack," she says.

He doesn't look at her. He *is* angry! He lied when he said he wasn't.

"Rachel," he says, softly, "honey? Let's get the bones. Okay? Let's put them away . . . where they can't . . . bones aren't . . . Jesus Christ." He slams his fist on the kitchen table. Rachel jumps. He covers his face with his hands. "Jesus Christ, Marla," he says.

Marla is Rachel's mother's name.

Rachel isn't sure what to do. She takes off her hat and coat. Then she walks into her bedroom and begins gathering the bones. After a while she realizes her father is standing in the doorway, watching.

Rachel hands her father all the bones. "Be careful," she says, "They killed Melinda." He doesn't say anything. That night he forgets to tell Rachel when to go to sleep. She changes into her pajamas, crawls into bed, and waits but he forgets to kiss her. He sits in the living room, making phone calls. The words drift into Rachel's room, "bones, mother murdered, lies, problems in school." Rachel thinks about Christmas. What will she get this year? Will she get a new Barbie? Will she get anything? Or has she been a bad girl? Will someone kill her father? Will Mrs. Williamson come to take care of her, and then lose her the way she lost the baby? Will Santa Claus save her? Will God? Will anyone? Will they get white lights for their tree or colored? Every year they switch but Rachel can't remember what they had last year. Rachel hopes it's a colored light year, because she likes the colored lights best. The last thing she hears before she falls asleep is her father's distant voice. "Bones," he says. "Yes that's right, bones."

The next morning, Rachel's father tells her she isn't going to school. She's going with him to Boston. "I made an appointment for you, okay, honey? I think you need a woman to talk to. So I made an appointment with Dr. Trentwerth."

Rachel is happy not to go to school with the nasty children of

Stone. She is happy not to have to sit in the classroom and listen to Mrs. Fizzure who never dresses like a Puritan and doesn't put anyone in the stockade or jail. Rachel is happy to go to Boston. They listen to Christmas music the whole way there. Rachel's appointment isn't until ten o'clock, so she has to sit in her dad's office and be very quiet while he does his work. He gives her paper and pens and she draws pictures of Christmas trees and ghosts while she waits. When it's time to go to her appointment, her father looks at her pictures and says, "These are very nice, Rachel." Rachel actually thinks they are sort of scary though she didn't draw the ghosts the way a kindergartner would, all squiggly lines and black spot eyes. She made them the way they really are, a lady smiling next to a Christmas tree, a baby asleep on a floor, a cat grinning.

Dr. Trentwerth has a long, gray braid that snakes down the side of her neck. She's wearing an orange sweater and black pants. Her earrings are triangles of tiny, gold bells. She says hello to Rachel's father but she doesn't shake his hand. She shakes Rachel's hand, as if she might be someone important. They leave her father sitting on the couch looking at a magazine.

Rachel is disappointed by the doctor's office. There are little kid toys everywhere. A stuffed giraffe, a dollhouse, blocks, trucks, and baby dolls with pink baby bottles. Rachel doesn't know what she's supposed to do. "Be polite," she remembers her father telling her.

"You have a nice room," Rachel says.

"Would you like some tea?" the doctor asks. "Or hot cocoa?"

Rachel walks past all the baby toys and sits in the chair by the window. "Cocoa please," she says.

Dr. Trentwerth turns the electric teakettle on. "Your father tells me you've been having some trouble with your bone collection," she says.

"He doesn't believe me."

"He said the bones hurt you."

Rachel nods. Shrugs. "But not all the time. Like I said. Just once."

The doctor tears open a packet of hot cocoa, which she empties into a plain white mug. She pours the water into it. "Let's just let that sit for a while," she says. "It's very hot. Whose bones hurt you, Rachel?"

Rachel sighs. "Cat bones, mice bones, chicken bones, you know."

Dr. Trentwerth nods. "Your father says you moved to Stone after your mother died. What was that like?"

"We were both really sad, me and Dad. Everyone was. We got a lot of flowers."

Dr. Trentwerth hands the mug to Rachel. "Careful, it's still hot."

Dr. Trentwerth is right. It is hot. Rachel brings it toward her mouth but it is too hot. She sets it, carefully, on the table next to the chair.

"Tell me about where you live," the doctor says as she sits down across from Rachel.

"Well, everyone is a witch," Rachel says. "Okay, not everyone, but almost everyone and one time, a long time ago, there was a woman there named Wilmot Redd and some people came and took her away 'cause they said all witches had to die. They hung her and no one did anything about it. Miss Engstrom, she was my teacher, got taken away too, and Melinda, my baby-sitter, died, but that's because she stole the bones and now my father has them and I don't want him to die but he probably will. Mrs. Williamson is this lady who sometimes takes care of me and she looks real nice but she loses babies and she lost one and no one even is looking for it. If my mom was still alive she would rescue me."

"And the bones?"

"They used to keep me company at night."

"Where would you be when the bones kept you company, Rachel?"

"In my room."

"In your bedroom?

"Mmhhm."

"I see."

"But then they stopped being nice and started hurting me."

"Whose bones, Rachel?"

"My dad has them now."

"Where did your dad's bones hurt you?"

"They were still mine then."

"Where did the bones hurt you, Rachel?"

"On my body."

"Where on your body?"

Suddenly, Rachel has a bad feeling. How does she know Dr. Trentwerth isn't one of them too? Rachel reaches for her mug and sips the hot cocoa. Dr. Trentwerth sits there, watching.

The moon is not a bone. Rachel knows this, but when the moon stares down at her, like an eye socket, Rachel wonders if she is just a small insect rattling around inside a giant skull. She knows this isn't true. She's not a baby, after all. She knows this isn't how reality works, but she can't help herself. Sometimes she imagines flying up to the moon, and climbing right through that hole to find everyone she's ever lost on the other side. She doesn't care about Melinda but she cares a lot about her mom and dad.

Rachel no longer lives in Stone and she no longer lives with her father. A lady and two policemen came to school one day and took Rachel away. She was cutting paper snowflakes at the time, and little bits of paper fluttered from her clothes as they walked to the car. Now Rachel lives with the Freemans. Big plastic candy canes line the walk up to the Freemans' front porch, which is decorated with blinking colored lights. A wreath with tiny gift-wrapped packages glued to it hangs on the front door. (But there are no gifts inside, Rachel checked.) The house smells sweet with the scent of holiday candles. Mrs. Freeman tells Rachel to be careful around the candles and not to bother Mr. Freeman when he is watching TV, which is most of the time.

Rachel's bedroom is in the back of the house. It has green, itchy carpet and two twin beds and a dresser that is mostly blue, with some patches of yellow and lime green, as though someone started to paint it and then gave up on the project. The curtains on Rachel's window are faded, tiny blue flowers with yellow centers and they are Rachel's favorite things in the room. Lying in her bed, Rachel can look out the window at the moon and imagine crawling right out of her world into a better one.

On the first night, Mrs. Freeman came into the bedroom and held Rachel while she cried and told her things would get better. In the morning, Mr. Freeman drove Rachel to school. He walked with a limp and he burped a lot, but before he left her in the school office he told her she was a brave girl and everything was going to be better soon.

"The Freemans are nice," the lady who took Rachel away from Stone told her. "Mrs. Freeman was once in the same situation you are in. She understands just what you're going through. And Mr. Freeman is a retired police officer. He got shot a few years ago. You're lucky to go there."

But Rachel didn't feel like a lucky girl, even when the Freemans took her to the Christmas tree lot and let her choose their tree, or when Mrs. Freeman put lotion on Rachel's chapped hands, or when they took her to an attorney's office, a very important woman who acted as if everything Rachel said mattered.

Rachel doesn't feel lucky until the day Mr. Freeman says, "Rachel, the lawyers think you should go back and live with your father." Mrs. Freeman cries and says, "Tomorrow's Christmas Eve, how can they do this?" But Rachel is so happy she almost pees in her pants. When the lady comes to pick Rachel up, Mrs. Freeman says, "I have half a mind not to let you take her." But Mr. Freeman says, "Rachel, get your suitcase." Mrs. Freeman hugs Rachel so tightly that for a second she is afraid she really isn't going to let her go, but then she does. The lady who waits for Rachel says, "This isn't my fault. This is hard for all of us." "It's hardest for her," Mrs. Freeman says and after that, Rachel doesn't hear the rest. Down the street the Mauley kids are building a snowman. "I hate you, George Mauley," Rachel screams at the top of her lungs. "What did you do that for?" the lady asks. "Get in the car." But Rachel has no idea why she did it. As they drive past the Mauley children, Rachel turns her face toward the window, so her back is to the lady. She sticks her tongue out at George Mauley but he is busy putting stones in the snowman's eyes and doesn't notice. "I want you to know, you are not alone," the woman says. "Maybe things didn't work out this time, but we are watching. You just keep telling the truth, Rachel, and I promise you things will get better."

It starts snowing. Not a lot, just tiny flakes fluttering down the white sky. Rachel remembers the snowflake she had been cutting when the lady took her away from Stone. What happened to her snowflake?

"Here we are then," the lady says. "Don't forget your suitcase." They walk into a big restaurant with orange booths along the wall and tiny Christmas trees on the tables. The waitresses wear brown dresses with white aprons and little half-circle hats that look like miniature spaceships crashed into all their heads. A woman is standing in one of the booths, waving and calling Rachel's name. The lady walks toward her. Rachel follows.

The woman wraps her arms around Rachel. She smells like soap. When she lets go of Rachel, she doesn't stand up but stays at Rachel's level, staring at her. Pink lipstick is smeared above her lips so she looks a little bit like she has three lips. Her eyebrows are drawn high on her forehead, beneath curls that are a strange shade of pink and orange, and she wears poinsettia earrings. "You remember me, don't you, honey?" she says. Then she looks up at the lady and frowns. "You can go now." She pulls Rachel close; together they pivot away from the lady. "Here, let me take that." She leans over and takes Rachel's suitcase. Rachel looks over her shoulder at the lady who is already walking away. "You don't remember me, do you? It's me. Grandma."

"Where's Dad?"

The Grandma sighs. "Are you hungry?" She guides Rachel into the booth and then slides in across from her. "This has all been expensive, you know. The lawyers and everything. He's at work. But he'll be home by the time we get there. Do you want a hamburger? A chocolate shake? What did you say to those people? Okay, I promised I wouldn't talk about it. Don't touch the little tree, Rachel, can't you just sit still for five minutes? It's just for looking."

Rachel's stomach feels funny. "Can I have an egg?"

"An egg? What kind of egg? Don't you want a hamburger?"

Rachel shakes her head. She starts to cry.

"Don't cry," the Grandma says. "It's over, all right? If you want an egg, you can have an egg. Were the people mean to you, Rachel? Did anyone hurt you?"

"Fried, please," Rachel says. "And can I have toast?"

"You can tell me, you know," the Grandma says. "Did anything happen to you while you were gone? Did anyone touch you in a bad way?"

Rachel is tired of the questions about bad touch. She is tired of grownups. Also she is cold. She just looks at the Grandma and after a while the Grandma says, "We decorated the tree last night. Your father hadn't even bought one yet. But don't worry; I set him straight about that. After everything you've been through! Well, he just wasn't thinking clearly. He's been through a lot too. Blue Spruce. It looks real nice."

The waitress comes and the Grandma orders a fried egg and toast for Rachel and the fish platter for herself. The waitress says, "Rachel?"

Miss Engstrom! Dressed as a waitress!

"Do you know each other?" the Grandma says.

"I used to be Rachel's teacher," Miss Engstrom says.

"In Boston?" asks the Grandma.

Miss Engstrom shakes her head, "No, in Stone. How are you, Rachel? Are you having a good holiday? Do you like your new teacher?"

"Wait, I know who you are. I know all about you."

"I wish you would come back," Rachel says.

"I forbid you to speak to my granddaughter, do you hear me? Where's the manager?"

Miss Engstrom's face does something strange, it sort of collapses, like an old Jack O' Lantern, but she shakes her head and everything goes back to normal. She smiles a fake smile at Rachel and walks away. The Grandma says, "She's the one who hurt you, isn't she? Where's that social worker when you need her? Why didn't you tell them about her, Rachel? Could you just tell me that?"

"Miss Engstrom never hurt me," Rachel says. "She was nice."

"Nice? She left bruises on your arms, Rachel."

Rachel sighs. She is *sooo* tired of stupid grownups and their stupid questions. "I told everyone," she says, "it wasn't her. It wasn't my dad, okay? It was the bones that did it."

"What bones? What are you talking about?"

But Rachel doesn't answer. She's learned a thing or two about answering adults' questions. Instead, she picks up the salt shaker and salts the table. The Grandmother grabs the shaker. "Just sit and wait for your egg," she says. "Maybe you could use this time to think about what you've done."

Rachel folds her hands neatly in front of her, just as she learned to do in Miss Engstrom's class. She is still sitting like that when Miss Engstrom returns with their order.

"You can eat now, Rachel," the Grandmother says. Rachel unfolds her hands and cuts her egg. The yellow yolk breaks open and smears across her plate. She can feel both Miss Engstrom and the Grandmother watching, but she pretends not to notice. The music is "Frosty the Snowman." Rachel eats her egg and hums along.

"Stop humming," says the Grandma, then, to Miss Engstrom, "You can go. We don't want anything else."

Miss Engstrom touches Rachel's head, softly. Rachel looks up at Miss Engstrom and sees that she is crying. Miss Engstrom nods at Rachel, one quick nod, as if they have agreed on something, then she sets the bill down on the table and walks away.

"Your father will be happy to see you," the Grandmother says. "Eat your egg. We've still got a long drive ahead of us."

Rachel's father does act happy to see her. He says, "I am so happy you are home," but he hugs her as if she is covered in mud and he doesn't want to get his clothes dirty.

The Christmas tree is already decorated. Rachel stares at it and the Grandma says, "Do you like it? We did it last night to surprise you." It is lit with tiny white lights, and oddly decorated with gold and white balls.

"Where are our ornaments?" Rachel asks.

"We decided to do something different this year," the Grandma says. "Don't you just love white and gold?"

Rachel doesn't know what to say. Clearly she is not expected to tell the truth. "Why don't you go unpack," the Grandma says, nodding at the suitcase. "Make yourself at home," she laughs.

Rachel is surprised, when she enters her bedroom, to discover that her bed is gone, replaced by two twin beds, just like at the Freemans'. One bed is covered with Rachel's old stuffed animals; they stare at her with their black eyes. She assumes this is her bed. Rachel inspects the animals and discovers that the ones she had cut open and stuffed with bones have been sewn shut, all except her white bear and he is missing. The other bed is covered with a pink lacy spread and several fat pillows. Next to it is a small table with a lamp, a glass of water, a few wadded tissues, and a stack of books.

"Surprise!" the Grandma says. "We're roomies now. Isn't this fun?"

Rachel nods. Apparently this is the right thing to do. The Grandma lifts the suitcase onto Rachel's bed. "Now, let's unpack your things and we can just forget about your little adventure and get on with our lives." The Grandma begins unpacking Rachel's suitcase, refolding the clothes before she puts them in the dresser. "Didn't anyone there help you with your clothes?" she says, frowning.

Rachel shrugs.

The Grandma closes the suitcase, clasps it shut, and puts it in the closet, right next to a set of plaid luggage. "Do you want a cookie? How about a gingerbread man? I've been baking up a storm, let me tell you."

Rachel follows the Grandma into the kitchen. *Baking up a storm?* she thinks. Maybe the Grandma is a witch; that would explain a lot. Her father is in the kitchen, talking on the phone, but when he sees her, he stops. He smiles at her, with the new smile of his and then he says, "She just walked into the kitchen. Can I call you back?" The Grandma is talking at the same time, something about chocolate chip eyes. Rachel's father says, "I love you too," softly, into the phone but Rachel stares at him in shock. Is he talking to her mother? Rachel knows that doesn't make sense. She's not a baby, after all, but who is he talking to?

"Here," the Grandma says, "choose."

Rachel looks down into the cookie tin the Grandma has thrust before her. Gingerbread men lie there with chocolate chip eyes and wrinkled red mouths. ("Dried cranberry," the Grandma says.) Rachel chooses the one at the top and immediately begins eating his face. Her father sits across from her and shakes his head when the Grandma thrusts the tin toward him. "I missed you," he says.

The gingerbread man is spicy but the eyes and nose are sweet. Rachel doesn't care for the mouth but that part is gone fast enough.

"Your grandmother has been nice enough to come here to live with us."

The Grandmother sets a glass of milk down in front of Rachel. "Oh, I was ready for a change. Who needs Milwaukee?"

Rachel doesn't know what to say about any of it. She chews her gingerbread man and drinks her milk. Her father and the Grandma seem to have run out of ideas as well. They simply watch her eat. When she's finished, she yawns and the Grandmother says, "Time for bed."

Rachel looks at her father, expecting him to do something. Just because she yawned doesn't mean she's ready for bed! But her father isn't any help.

"Say good night," the Grandma says.

"Good night," says Rachel. She gets up, pushes the chair in, and rinses her glass. The Grandma follows her into the bedroom. She stays there the whole time Rachel is getting undressed. Rachel feels embarrassed but she doesn't know what else to do, so she pretends she doesn't mind the Grandma sitting on her bed talking about how much fun it's going to be to share the room. "Every night just like a slumber party," she says. After Rachel goes to the bathroom, brushes her teeth, and washes her face and hands, the Grandma tells her to kneel by her bed. The Grandma, complaining the whole time about how difficult it is, kneels down beside her.

"Lord," she says. "Please help Rachel understand right from wrong, reality from imagination, truth from lies and all that. Thank you for sending her home. Do you have anything to add? Rachel?"

Rachel can't think of anything to say. She shakes her head. The Grandma makes a lot of noise as she stands up again.

Rachel crawls into bed and the Grandma tucks the covers tight. So tight that Rachel feels like she can't breathe, then the Grandma kisses Rachel's forehead and turns out the light. Rachel waits, for a long time, for her father to come in to kiss her good night but he never does.

It is very dark when Rachel wakes up. The room is dark and

there is no light shining under the door. It takes a moment for Rachel to realize why she's woken up. A soft rustling sound is coming from the closet.

"Grandma?" Rachel whispers, and then, louder, "Grandma?"

The Grandma wakes up, sputtering, "Marla? Is that you?"

"No. It's me, Rachel. Do you hear that noise?"

They listen for a while. It seems, to Rachel, a very long time and she is just starting to worry that the Grandma will think she is lying when the rustling starts again.

"We've got a mouse," the Grandma says. "Don't worry, I have a feeling Santa Claus might bring you a cat this year."

Very soon the Grandma is snoring in her bed. The rustling sound stops and then, just as Rachel is falling asleep, starts again. Rachel stares into the dark with burning eyes. It doesn't matter what the grownups do, she realizes, she's not safe anywhere.

Carefully, Rachel feels around in the dark for her bunny slippers. She picks up a shoe by mistake, and is startled by how large it is until she realizes it must belong to the Grandmother. She sets it down and picks up first one slipper, and then the other.

Her bunny slippers on, Rachel tiptoes out of the bedroom into the hallway, which is softly lit by the white glow of the Sheekles' Christmas-light reindeer. Rachel isn't sleepwalking, she is completely awake, but she feels strange, as though somehow she is both entirely awake and asleep at the same time. Rachel feels like she hears a voice calling from a great distance. But she isn't hearing it with her ears; it's more like a feeling inside, a feeling inside and outside of herself too. This doesn't make sense, Rachel knows, but this is what is happening. Maybe the grownups aren't right about anything, about what is real, or what is possible.

When she walks outside, the bitter cold hits Rachel hard. But she does not go back to her warm bed, instead she walks in the deadly dark of Stone, lit by occasional Christmas lights, and the few cars from which she hides, all the way to Old Burial Hill where the graves stand in the oddly blue snow, marking the dead who once lived there.

Rachel isn't afraid. She lies down. It is cold. Well, of course it is. She shivers, staring up at the stars, which, come to think of it, look like chips of bones. Maybe the skull she's been trapped in has been smashed open by some giant child who is, even now, searching through the pieces, hoping to find her. She closes her eyes.

"No, no. Not your bones. You've misunderstood everything."

Rachel opens her eyes. Standing before her is the old woman.

"Get up. Stamp your feet."

Rachel just lies there so the woman pulls her up.

"Are you a witch?" Rachel asks.

"Clap your hands and stamp your feet."

"Are you real?"

But the old woman is gone and Rachel's father is running toward her. "What are you doing here?" he says. "Rachel, what is happening to you?"

He wraps her tight in his arms and picks her up. One of her bunny slippers falls from her foot and lands softly on the snow-covered grave but he doesn't notice. He is running down the hill. Rachel, bouncing in his arms, watches the bunny slipper get smaller and smaller. She holds her father tight.

The Grandma is waiting for them in the kitchen where she is heating milk on the stove. She has on a flowered robe; her pinky-red hair, sparkling in the light, circles her face like a clown.

"She was in the graveyard," Rachel's father says.

The Grandma touches Rachel's bare arm with her own icy fingers. "Get a blanket. She's chilled to the bone."

Rachel's father sets her on the kitchen chair. He gently pries her fingers from around his neck. "I'll be right back," he says. "You have to let me go."

Rachel watches the doorway until he returns, carrying the white comforter from his bed. He wraps Rachel in it ("like a sausage," he used to say in happier times) then sits down with her on his lap.

Rachel's father kisses her head. She starts to feel warm. "Rachel," her father says, "never do that again. We'll visit your mother's grave in Boston more often, if that's what you want, but don't just leave in the middle of the night. Don't scare us like that."

Rachel nods. The Grandmother hands her a Santa Claus-face mug of hot chocolate, and sets another on the table in front of Rachel's father.

Rachel sips her hot chocolate, gives the Grandma a close look.

"Good, isn't it?" the Grandma says.

Rachel nods.

"Milk. That's the secret ingredient. None of that watery stuff."

The Grandmother sets the tin of gingerbread men on the table and Rachel reaches for one, teetering on her father's lap. He hands her a gingerbread man and takes one for himself.

"Well, it's a good thing you didn't fall asleep out there," the Grandma says.

Rachel swallows the gingerbread foot. "I started to but someone woke me up. I think it was that witch, Wilmot Redd. She found me and she made me stand up. She told me she didn't want my bones."

Rachel's father and the Grandmother look at each other. Rachel stops chewing and stares straight ahead, waiting to see if her father will make her get off his lap or if the Grandma will call the lady to come and take her away again.

"Rachel, Wilmot Redd was just some old lady. A fisherman's wife," Rachel's father says, gently.

The Grandma sits down at the kitchen table. She looks at Rachel so hard that Rachel finally has to look back at her. The Grandma's face is extraordinarily white and Rachel thinks it looks just a little bit like a paper snowflake.

"I think I know who it might have been," she says, "Have you ever heard of La Befana? She's an old woman. Much older than me. And scary looking. Ugly. She carries around a big, old sack filled with gifts that she gives to children. A long time ago the three wise men stopped by her house to get directions to Bethlehem, to see the Christ Child, you know. And after she gave them directions they invited her along but she didn't go with them 'cause she had too much housework to do. Of course she immediately regretted being so stupid and she's been trying to catch up ever since, so she goes around giving gifts to all the children just in case one of them is the Savior she neglected to visit, all those years ago, just 'cause she had dirty laundry to take care of. I bet that's who helped you tonight. Old La Befana herself." The Grandmother turns to look at Rachel's father. "It's about time this family had some luck, right? And what could be luckier than to be part of a real live Christmas miracle?"

Rachel's father hugs her and says, "Well, this little miracle better go to bed. Tomorrow is Christmas Eve, you don't want to sleep through it, do you?"

The Grandmother takes the mug of hot chocolate and the half-eaten gingerbread man from Rachel. Her father carries her to bed, tucks her in, and kisses her forehead. Rachel is falling asleep, listening to the faint murmuring voices of her father and the Grandmother, when she hears the noise. She goes to the closet, opens it, and sees right away, the Halloween treat bag in the corner, rustling as though the mouse is trapped inside. She is just about to shut the door when the small hand reaches out of the bag, grasps the paper edge, and another hand appears, and then, a tiny, bone head.

"Is that you?" Rachel whispers.

The bones don't answer. They just come walking toward her, their sharp points squeaking.

Rachel slams the closet door shut. She runs out of her room. The Grandma and her father are sitting next to the tree. When they turn to her, their faces are flicked with yellow, blue and green, they grin the wide skeletal grin of skulls. "Honey, is something the matter?" her father asks. Rachel shakes her head. "Are you sure? You look like you've seen —"

The Grandma interrupts, "Is it the mouse? Did you see the mouse?"

Rachel nods.

"Don't worry about it," the Grandma says, "Maybe Santa Claus will bring you a kitty this year."

Rachel refuses to go back to bed until her father and the Grandmother walk with her. They tuck her in, and again her father kisses her forehead, and the Grandma does the same, and then they leave her alone in the dark. After a while she hears the bones squeaking across the floor. Rachel feels around in the dark until she finds the Grandmother's big shoe. Rachel waits until she hears the squeaking start once more. When it does, she pounds where the sound comes from, and the first two times, she hits only the floor but the next five or six, she hears the breaking of bones, the small cries and curses. Her father and Grandmother run into the room and turn on the light. "Well, you killed it," the Grandma says, looking at her, strangely. "I'll go get the broom and dustpan."

Rachel's father doesn't say anything. They just stand there, looking at the mess on the floor, and then at the mess on the bottom of the Grandmother's shoe.

Later, after it's all cleaned up, Rachel crawls back into bed. She pulls the blankets to her chin, and rolls to her side. Her father and the Grandmother stand there for a while before they walk out of the room. For a long time Rachel listens in the dark but all she hears is her own breathing, and she falls asleep to the comforting sound.

When she wakes again it is Christmas Eve and snowing outside, glistening white flakes that tumble down the sky from the snow queen's garden, the Grandma says.

Because it is a special day the Grandma lets Rachel have gingerbread cookies and hot chocolate for breakfast on the couch while her father sleeps late. "He's worn out after everything you've been through," the Grandma says. Occasionally Rachel thinks she hears mewing from her father's room but the Grandma says, "Anyone can sound like a cat. It's probably just a sound he makes in his sleep. You, for instance, last night you were singing in your sleep."

"I was?" Rachel asks.

"Didn't anyone ever tell you that before? You sing in your sleep."

"I do?"

The Grandma nods. "You're a very strange little girl, you know," she says.

Rachel chews the gingerbread face and sighs.

"Now what do you suppose this is all about?"

The Grandma stands next to the Christmas tree, looking out the window. Rachel gets off the couch and squeezes between the Grandma and the tree. A gray cat meanders down the crooked sidewalk in front of the house. In its mouth it holds a limp mouse. Walking behind the cat is a straggling line of children in half-buttoned winter coats and loosely tied scarves, tiptoeing in boots and wet sneakers, not talking to each other or catching snowflakes on their tongues, only intently watching the cat with their bright eyes.

"Like the Pied Piper," the Grandma says.

Rachel shrugs and goes back to the couch. "It's just a bunch of the little kids," she says. "Who's the Pied Piper?"

The Grandma sighs. "Don't they teach you anything important these days?"

Rachel shakes her head.

"Well, it looks like I'll have to," the Grandma says.

And she does.

Two thousand copies of this book have been printed by the Maple-Vail Book Manufacturing Group, York, PA, for Golden Gryphon Press, Urbana, IL. The typeset is Electra with Palette display, printed on 55# Sebago. Typesetting by The Composing Room, Inc., Kimberly, WI.